LIVING WITH
MONSTERS

LIVING WITH MONSTERS

RORY BARNES

GLADIATOR PRESS

First edition
Published in Great Britain in 2005 by
Gladiator Press
Little Water House
The Homestall
Ashurst Wood
East Grinstead
Sussex
RH19 3PQ
01342 823769
gladiator@littlewater.freeserve.co.uk

A catalogue record for this book is available from the
British Library.

ISBN 0-9550282-0-5

Printed and bound by The Ink Pot Lithographic Printers,
Southborough, Tunbridge Wells, Kent TN4 0LT

CONTENTS

MY BLOOD BROTHER

CHAPTER 1

It hasn't been easy having a vampire for a brother. Mind you it didn't start like that. I mean he'd always been a vampire, but it didn't sort of show 'til later. In fact, until he was fourteen, my brother Josh was just like any other boy.

By that, I mean he was a right pain in the butt. At least that's what I thought at the time, but then I was sixteen and Josh kept getting in the way. You know the sort of thing, borrowing my clothes, which suddenly started to fit him, and wanting to join in with me and my friends.

"Josh," I said. "Just because you're spoiled rotten by Mum and Dad doesn't mean you can do what you want with me, so get a life and make your own friends." And after a while Josh did. Not that that worried me. I'd seen him eye up my girlfriend and that was enough for me. Brother Josh could go and get any sort of life, anywhere, so long as it wasn't too near me.

So it was that I didn't really notice that Josh was keeping himself to himself, more and more. I didn't think about it until Dad mentioned it to me one evening. "Eg," he said, "Josh seems very preoccupied. Is anything the matter with him?"

Eg, I ask you, what sort of a name is that. Eg is for Egbert. And how did they do that to me? Don't answer. There is no answer. I love my Dad and my

Mum, which is just as well. Egbert ! And then what name does Josh get!

Anyway, by the time I'd got to the ripe old age of sixteen and Dad asked about Josh I'd got used to my name. "I'll have a chat with him" I said, and went off to do Dad's job for him. After all, I don't see why he couldn't have asked Josh himself.

Since you are, or should, be wondering how my brother was a vampire and I was not, I will explain. Josh and I were adopted. You'll want to know about Josh I suppose. Well, you'll have to hear about me first. There's not a lot of it. I was found in a basket apparently, on some steps outside a Church. One of my parents, perhaps both of them, must have been fair. I think one of them must have had a spot problem when young. Sometimes I try to imagine what they were like, him tall and spotty and her fair-haired. Perhaps it was the other way round. More than likely they both had spots.

Now Josh, you've guessed it, had a skin like a peach, brown skin, and black hair and long black eyelashes, and he had long white teeth as I expect you also guessed but we'll go into that later.

I'll never know what caused my parents, or more probably just my mother, to leave me in a basket. I'm sure it was for the best of reasons. I suppose my mother must have been a churchgoer. I mean, she could have left me outside a police station or public library or something like that couldn't she.

My brother Josh wasn't left to fend for himself in a basket. Josh exploded into adoption, quite literally. His parents were killed in a gas explosion. I didn't get the gory details until later, and by then I could see how it had all happened.

I daresay you've thought of the question haven't you? Vampires are supposed to live forever, so how did Josh become an orphan? Well, fate took a hand, as they say. Josh's mother was right in the middle of the explosion, and they found hardly anything at all of her afterwards. As for Josh's father, a leg of a kitchen chair got blown right through him. Through where, you're thinking. Yes, that's it. Zap, right through the heart.

What a bit of bad luck for a vampire, and for Josh too. Although it wasn't such bad luck in some ways. Josh's family had been poor, originating from a distant country of poor people and unpleasant things like hunger and disease (and apparently vampires). All this, at a stroke or rather after an explosion, Josh exchanged for a comfortable upbringing with three televisions, a DVD recorder and lots of other goodies. He also got Mum and Dad and me. What did I get? I got Josh.

CHAPTER 2

I've learned a lot about vampires since Josh turned into one. I used to think I knew all the rules about them, but I can tell you some of them are exaggerated. For example, vampires don't live forever, just for a long time; and they can be killed, although it's very difficult. And they can go out in the daylight, although sunshine makes them feel ill.

Looking back, perhaps the first sign was when Josh puked up his favourite meal. This was rabbit stew. I know some people don't like the idea of eating rabbit. It reminds them of pets, but we didn't think of it like that. Josh loved rabbit stew. Mum cooked it with cider and garlic. We hadn't had it for months and Josh pigged out on it, but not for long. Just a few bites, and he went as white as a bag of flour. Out of the room he dashed, and we could hear sick noises down the hall through the lavatory door. Yes, that must have been the start of it. Vampires don't like garlic. If someone tells you that, it's true. Take my word for it.

So it was that I wandered in to Josh's room one evening shortly after Dad had his word with me. Josh was peering at himself in the mirror with an anxious look on his face. Aha, thought I, can Josh be getting spots? This cheering idea fluttered away when Josh turned to me and said, "Come and look at this, Eg." No being startled, no guilty shame at spot picking, no surprise that I had come into his room

12

when I usually avoided him if I could. This was clearly something serious.

Standing by Josh's side I peered into the mirror above his desk. Then I took off my glasses and gave them a good wipe. Then I gave the mirror a firm wipe with my arm. Then I looked at Josh and then back at the mirror.

In the glass was my own too familiar face; long, fair haired, spotty and with a look of horrified fascination. By its side was a pattern of shifting light, a reflection of Josh's face as in a pool of water with stones thrown into it. This image seemed to break up into different coloured triangles, shifting like a kaleidoscope, and sometimes parts of it would vanish completely. But occasionally the shifting lights would stop, and there by the side of my mystified face would be Josh's, staring at me with fear and panic in his eyes.

Poor old Josh. I don't think I'd ever felt sorry for him before but I did now. I wasn't sure what I was sorry about, but whatever this thing was it was very peculiar, and it was really scaring Josh.

It scared me too. "What on earth is it?" I said.
"I don't know," he said. "It's been going on for two or three weeks and it's getting worse. It's a lot worse today."
"Maybe it's the mirror," I said. But Josh shook his head.
"It's every mirror," he replied.

13

"We'd better ask Dad," I said, but Josh grabbed my arm.

"No," he said. "No one must know. No one."

I should have known better, shouldn't I? I should have patted Josh on the back, got out of his room as quickly as possible and left this problem to better people than I. I should have got the hell out of it. What did I do? I put my arm round this little monster's shoulder and said, "Don't you worry, we'll sort it out." And then I took the mirror off the wall. "You won't be needing this," I said. "You can swap it for one of my posters". And I left his room with the mirror under my arm and Josh's problem on my shoulders.

CHAPTER 3

The next day was Friday, and a wonderful sunny spring day it was, the sort that either makes you feel really good or that all your clothes are old and tatty. I was feeling really good. At least I was until I woke Josh up. He hadn't appeared by 8 o'clock and I could see he was going to be late for school. Why should I bother?

Anyway, I went into Josh's bedroom. "Up you get, lazy bones" I said, and pulled back the curtains. But instead of blinking at the sudden sunlight pouring all over him, Josh cried out. He curled up in a ball, his hands clasped over his head. Then he opened his eyes, looking between his fingers, and then shot out of bed, grabbed the curtains and pulled them shut violently so his hands banged together.

Josh turned on me. "Never, never, never do that to me again, Eg". He rubbed his hands over his face as if he was wiping something unpleasant away.
"But you'll be late for school," I said.

A more sensible person would have gone on ahead and left Josh to be late on his own. What was my reward? Josh shambling beside me, head down, dark glasses on and his coat collar turned up. Once we got on the bus I let Josh go upstairs first and then I sat downstairs. There are limits to brotherly love.

You might think that by now I would have realised what was happening. But then you don't expect your brother to turn into a vampire do you. I mean, if your sister started barking like a dog at night and getting into red meat you wouldn't immediately think she was becoming a werewolf would you. More likely you'd send her off to the doctor.

In fact, that's what we did with Josh eventually. But I'm getting ahead of myself. I mentioned red meat and that was the next thing with Josh. It was his birthday and we went out to the Steak House. Josh loved a T-bone steak and liked it well done. Dad always went on at him about how it cooked all the goodness out but that was how Josh liked it. But not today. When the waitress asked how he wanted his steak he looked a bit embarrassed and said he'd have it rare, very rare. Dad made some joke about Josh becoming a man at last. He didn't know how wrong he was; becoming a vampire more like. Still he found out soon enough.

We clocked it at last one Friday evening when Mum and Dad had gone out. Josh and I had clubbed together for a DVD and a Chinese take-away from down the road. We cooked our own rice and I sliced up some tomatoes as a salad. Half way through I sliced my finger.

"Ouch," I said, and turned round, holding my cut finger. You know how much blood you can get out of a cut finger, and this dripped over my hands and onto the floor. "Josh" I shouted through the kitchen doorway. "Get me some plaster, I've cut myself."

Josh came in with the plasters and stopped in his tracks. He just stood and stared at me, or rather at my cut finger and the blood. His eyes widened, his nostrils flared and he breathed in deeply. I could see he was opening and closing his hands, stretching his fingers as if he wanted to get at something. Then he gave a dreadful unJoshlike smile, baring his teeth, and promptly snapped his mouth shut. He put his hand over his mouth. For a few moments we just stared at one another. Then Josh threw the plaster box at me, spun round and left the room.

The food was on the plates already, so I plastered myself up and without bothering to clear up the kitchen marched into the living room with the tray. Josh was sunk silently into an armchair. I passed his plate to him. "Shall we watch the DVD?" I said. Silence. I've had enough of this, I thought. I get the meal, get the DVD, get my hand cut and he goes into a sulk. I pressed the remote control.

And what was this video about, I hear you ask. Yes, that's it. It was about vampires. At first, things went normally. Mist swirled, the undead crawled out of his grave, Josh and I chomped on our sweet and sour. Then the beautiful victim was saved by a necklace of garlic wrapped round her neck and Josh put his spoon down. Next came a really gross bit and much slurping of blood, heard in our room of dead silence. Finally, the hero was shaving, looking at himself in the mirror and, turning round, found to his surprise the vampire standing right behind him.

The surprise was because the vampire was in front of the mirror but could not be seen in it.

A dreadful cry came from poor Josh. "Noooooo". He dashed up to the T.V. set, switched it off and stood in front of it as if he was hiding the screen and its message to both of us. His chest heaved up and down. "I'm a vampire!" he said. "I'm becoming a vampire!" And he ran into the kitchen and closed the door.

For a while I continued eating my take-away, but my mind was working overtime and, for all I tasted the food, I might as well have been eating grass. So I put my plate down and went into the kitchen.

There, on his hands and knees, was Josh. Praying? No definitely not praying and you can have another half dozen guesses because you won't get it. Or maybe you have.

There was Josh, licking the floor. This wasn't a new and sudden approach to tidying up. Josh had never been much good at that although he did have certain talents when it came to making a mess. No, Josh was licking up the congealed blood of you- know- who. When I came in he looked up just as he was licking his lips.

Now it's bad enough to find your brother may be a vampire. But to have him look at you like a dog at the Sunday joint is really weird, I can assure you. And frightening. I looked at the table and sure enough the bloodstained tomato had gone and in its place sat the kitchen knife, clean and shining with no trace of blood; freshly cleaned not to say freshly licked.

Josh got up from the floor. He wiped his mouth with his fingers and then carefully licked them. "I feel much better," he said. That's more than could be said for me. I felt worse, much worse.

However, Josh certainly looked a lot better. Over the previous months he'd been going downhill steadily and getting very tired, particularly in the day. But the nasty grey look he'd developed had gone.

"It's the blood," he said. "The blood. I wonder if animal blood does the same." Then he caught me by the arm. "Let's go to your room," he said. And we did, and Josh took his old mirror from the back of my wardrobe. We admired my face in this, a very worried and white face. But of Josh there was no sign at all.

CHAPTER 4

It could have been worse I suppose. Just imagine if Josh had been a vegetarian. At least he didn't have that to worry about. But there were plenty of other things.

Mirrors were the first problem. I hadn't realised how much difficulty Josh had dodging them. The one in the hall was the most dangerous. I solved that, temporarily at least, by accidentally smashing it. That cost me a fine from my pocket money. Josh contributed, I hear you say. Did he? Not likely.

In fact life got very expensive. I didn't realise how much meat cost. Mum got more and more worried about Josh. Although he started to look better it seemed to her that he was right off his food. She kept on talking about anorexia. But then she didn't know Josh was secretly gorging himself on cheap cuts of raw meat. When I say cheap I really mean less expensive. I don't recommend keeping a vampire as a pet unless you're rich.

Blood was the difficult thing. Have you ever gone into a butchers and asked for a pint of blood. I have, and take my advice, don't bother. I tried several times without any luck. I gave up when one butcher called out to his assistant, "'Ere Charlie, we've got Count Dracula wiv an order." I was tempted to send Josh out one evening to bite the horrible man. What a thought to have. I wouldn't let it enter my mind now. Not after all the trouble we had with Josh biting people.

At this stage Josh's liking for a quick nip hadn't shown itself. If I'd really thought, I could have seen the problems ahead. "Animal blood is OK," said Josh. "But it's human blood that really gets me going. I felt so well when I had that stuff from your finger." Why didn't he come out with it. I want to drink your blood, brother dear. Josh continued, "You know, something very curious happened to my teeth, my eye teeth, the ones either side in the front. They've got really sharp, and when I smelt that blood they seemed to get longer as well."

What do you think is the stupidest thing I could do now? What would send creepy feelings down your back? What wouldn't you do for anyone and especially not for your gross younger brother ?

I heated the needle to kill any germs. When it was cool I pricked my finger. Easy to say isn't it. Not so easy to do. It's one thing to accidentally cut yourself, but quite another to start chopping on purpose. So I gave up that idea. Instead, I pulled the plaster off my old cut, which hadn't completely healed, and messed around with it until I got some blood out onto a white saucer.

Then as arranged I called Josh in. He entered with a hideous smile, showing his teeth so we could see what happened to them. The effect was extraordinary. There wasn't so much blood this time so Josh had to get quite near to the saucer. But then the nostrils flared and the teeth really did get bigger. They sort of slid out, just the canine teeth, the pointed ones at the side.

When Josh had finished licking the saucer he said, "Thank you Eg." I was feeling pretty gloomy by now. I had a vision of myself covered all over with plasters from providing meals for Josh.

"I suppose you won't be able to go to Church either," I said. After all, every vampire film I've ever seen has the thing running away from crosses and such like. Josh had already thought of this. Why I don't know since he never goes willingly to Church.

"No problem" he said. "I've been into several churches to see." I hoped he'd been praying for someone to come and sort all this out. I certainly had.

CHAPTER 5

I'd better tell you a bit about our Dad because he comes into the story now. Dad had a business buying and selling things from and to other countries. He had an office, and a warehouse on the other side of town. Dad didn't look like a business man though, more like a mad professor, and he had long wild hair which was going grey. He was very tall and thin and friendly, except when he flew off the handle, which was every day.

I could see Dad was going to have to know. I kept rehearsing how to tell him. By the way Dad, Josh is a vampire. Or, now Dad I've got bad news for you. Or, what do you think about vampires Dad? I spent a lot of time worrying about this.

And what about Josh? Josh was cheerful. "Let me do the worrying Josh," I had said in a moment of weakness. And he did. And I did.

At least Josh knew what the problem was. And that was a lot less worrying for him than seeing his reflection in the mirror disappearing day by day without reason. I suppose that was why he was cheerful.

The strain was beginning to tell on me, however. I was preoccupied at school. I couldn't invite my friends round any more. I was becoming a hermit, locked up with Josh. My girlfriend Susan began to complain.

While I was still thinking of ways to tell Dad, fate took a hand again. We had two upstairs bathrooms in our house, one on the landing and one leading from Mum and Dad's bedroom. One Saturday morning Mum was out shopping and Dad was off somewhere else. Josh and I had a lie in. I got up about 10 a.m. and went to the bathroom. Knock knock, Josh wanted to come in. "Get lost!" I shouted.

"O.K. I'll go to the other one," he said. Shortly afterwards I heard the back door open, and Dad thumping up the stairs. Then a knock on the other bathroom door and Dad's voice: "Hurry up, whoever you are, I'm bursting."

Then there was a long silence. As I opened my bathroom door Josh went past. He was silent and white. He didn't look at me. I went into Mum and Dad's bedroom. Dad was sitting on the bed looking dazed. Looking through the bathroom door I could see the full length mirror inside, facing it. Forgetful, Josh must have opened the door while standing in front of the mirror.

I cleared my throat nervously. "Er, what do you think about vampires Dad?"

Perhaps I could have explained things better. Anyway, after a while Dad sort of got the idea. He took it quite well really, and it went off better than it might have done. I don't think anyone in the street heard the shouting. And he didn't hurt Josh at all, just frightened him a bit. It didn't take long to clear up the broken things although Josh's door didn't get fixed until the following week.

After he'd calmed down Dad walked round the house muttering to himself. I could hear occasional words. "God almighty .... what shall I say to Sarah" (my Mother)".... all I need right now .... thank God when they've all left home .... last straw", and so on.

I went to my room but was disturbed by a crash of broken glass in the garden. Looking out of my window I saw Dad waving a hammer over the dustbin. I went into Mum and Dad's bathroom. The big mirror had been taken off the wall. As I went downstairs I saw that every mirror in the house had been removed.

Dad came into the kitchen. He kept clasping his head and his hair stood on end. "Get Josh," he said.

We sat round the table. Josh and I drank coffee and Dad had opened a bottle of whisky. Please don't get the idea I also suffered from alcoholic parents but he liked a drink from time to time and he was under a lot of strain.

"We've got to stick together chaps," he said. "We'll work it out. Don't you worry." He drank another glass. "It's not your fault Josh. You've had to put up with a lot." He took another gulp.

No thanks for poor old Eg, you note. Still a trouble shared is a trouble halved, as they say. I began to feel a bit better.

25

"I'll have to tell your Mother" Dad said. Just then her car drew up in the drive. Josh and I shot upstairs to my room. And there we stayed, viewing the events from the window and hearing muffled sounds from the kitchen.

It wasn't long before we heard Mum laughing. After that there was some shouting, mostly from Dad. Then I saw Dad go into the garden and rummage in the dustbin. He came back with a bit of mirror. Then Dad came and took Josh downstairs. On his return Josh told me Dad made him stand in front of the broken piece of mirror. When Josh came back we could hear Mum crying in the kitchen for a while and then silence.

After a while Dad came up again. He had a plaster on his hand and he took Josh downstairs. Apparently Dad had put some of his own blood on a plate and Josh was made to show how the vampire teeth worked. Josh wanted to lick up the blood afterwards. Dad told him where to go, but Mum persuaded him to let Josh have the dish. By the time Josh got back to my room the dish was clean and Josh's eyes were sparkling.

Josh and I kept ourselves to ourselves for the rest of the day. Mum went out again in the car and came back with some shopping. Then Dad went out and returned with a pile of books under each arm. No need to wonder what those were about. At about 6.30 mum called out, "Supper!". We all sat down as if nothing had happened. Then the food was served up, steak and chips. Except that Josh's steak was raw. The whisky bottle was on the table. I noticed that it was half empty. Mum sloshed some into her glass and into Dad's. Then she made a great fuss of pouring me out a glass of cider. Finally she disappeared and came back with a pint mug which she plonked by Josh. Then she sat at the table and started eating, her head down.

This was a strange meal I thought. Stranger still that I had a glass of cider pressed on me. Even stranger that Josh was given what appeared to be a pint of red wine. It took a while for my slow brain to realise that Mum had given Josh a pint of blood. Obviously she was better than I at handling butchers.

So there we were. All nice and cosy. Mum and Dad had come to the rescue. Everything was going to be alright and Eg's life was going to get back to normal. Except that things got worse.

CHAPTER 6

At first things went well enough. It wasn't back to normal exactly, but near normal. I even invited Susan round. Not to a meal, you understand. Can you imagine it. Would you like a glass of blood Susan? No thank you, and goodbye!

Mum was wonderful. She just acted as if nothing was wrong. I'd better tell you about Mum now. She was very beautiful, about five feet nine and blonde and a bit vague. At least she seemed vague but she got an amazing amount done. She worked teaching handicapped children, looked after us, and kept Dad under control. Those were no small things, especially the last two.

After two or three days Dad brought the subject up over supper. "I've read everything I can find about this, this ... thing," he said. "And a fine load of rubbish I've had to plough through. However, there's clearly something in it since we have Josh here how he is. It's something in the blood." Who would have thought of that! Surely Dad could do better than this.

Dad continued. "If it is the blood then there may be a cure. I think we should send Josh to the doctor."
I said, "But Dad, what will we say to the doctor? We can hardly say Josh is a vampire can we?"
"No, we'll say he feels unwell, listless, that we're worried he may be anaemic." Dad looked at Mum for agreement and she nodded her head vigorously. A

lot of good that would be, I thought. And I was right. Josh did all right out of it. Dad went spare.

The doctor examined Josh. He said he seemed a bit pale, which was understandable since Josh never went outside in the day if he could avoid it. He said Josh was a bit unfit, which was true since Josh had had to give up all sporting activities because most changing rooms have big mirrors in them. He advised Josh to get out in the open air and take up a sport, jogging perhaps. Very helpful. Night-time jogging maybe.

However, pressed by Mum, who went with Josh, the doctor sent him up to the hospital for a blood test. Mum took time off and she and Josh waited for an hour before Josh was called in to see the technician. Now I'm not making this up, really I'm not, but apparently the technician got called away and left Josh alone in a room full of tubes of blood. Well it wasn't surprising Josh did it, is it? I mean, you might as well leave a drunk in charge of an off-licence. Apparently there was a dreadful fuss afterwards went they found so many specimens had gone but no one thought to blame Josh.

Mum knew something was up as soon as she saw Josh come out. She said it was as if he was walking on air. He was as high as a kite.

Dad really pitched into him. "It's bad enough to ask other people to touch your wretched blood and risk becoming vampires," he said. "But it can work the other way. Why do you think those samples had

29

been taken if it wasn't to find out if people were ill. Lord knows what you may have caught. It's no joke. What about Aids." Another Aids Lecture I thought, but I could see what he meant.

Josh didn't sicken. The test results arrived and he and Mum went to the Doctor. The Doctor said Josh's blood was OK, A1, healthy and vigorous. He didn't know how vigorous.

The next thing was we started to go to church. We used to go once or twice a year. Now it was every Sunday and no nonsense. I think it was Mum's idea. Dad had tried the doctor, now she was going to try the church.

Of course, Josh and I knew he'd be all right in church but Mum and Dad didn't. It only occurred to me afterwards that we could have told them. I remember how we drew up outside the church for the first time and got out and how Mum and Dad kept looking anxiously at Josh. It reminded me of a film I saw where a little boy possessed by the devil struggles to avoid being carried into church. I think Mum and Dad were afraid Josh might go like that but he didn't. Josh just stood there singing away like an angel. More like a bat really.

Josh didn't change into a bat I can reassure you. What he did learn to do was to control his teeth. First he found he could make them slide out without seeing blood. He said he just imagined the blood. The second trick, and the more difficult one, was making the teeth go back when he had blood in front of him. Yes, you know whose blood. Not Josh's for sure. Still it was worth the effort. If Josh was to survive outside a zoo or laboratory he had to be able to avoid giving himself away. So we had tooth control practices. I'd wave a saucer with a bit of blood at Josh and he'd see if he could get the teeth back where they belonged.

Josh and I tried to beat the mirror problem. We covered bits of him with make-up, paint, silver foil and anything else we could think of. As soon as any of it touched Josh it vanished in the mirror. There was no logic to it. You would have thought his clothes and so on would have shown. Still as Josh said it was best that way. A complete absence of Josh's reflection was one thing. Josh's clothes with no head or hands would have been quite another.

At one point I thought I'd found the answer. If Josh drank his own blood that would be it. It would go round and round in a never ending circle and cause no one any trouble. Not a bad idea was it. In fact I thought it was brilliant. The next step was to get some of it. Not an easy task. When I think how I've chopped myself up to provide blood for Josh it makes me despair of him. In the end I grabbed his finger and stuck the pin in it myself. And what a howl he made. Josh was definitely a taker rather than a giver of blood. After all that he didn't like it. "I'd rather have a piece of pig's liver any day," he said.

I did wonder if he was faking so as to avoid a life of pricking his own fingers. But no, there was no light in his eyes the way there was after other people's blood. He couldn't fake that.

So where did this get us all? How did we feel? Dad was working overtime on it. He kept coming back with more books. He made more plans. He didn't talk to us about it but we could hear him going on and on at Mum about it after they had gone to bed. How was Mum? Determined I'd say. And me? I thought things were going to get better. What a moron. And Josh? Well what do you think? Josh was in fine spirits, if that's the word to use.

CHAPTER 7

Our new life developed. Some people at school took the piss out of Josh for wearing dark glasses and so on, but a lot of people thought it was cool, especially some of the girls.

Not surprisingly Josh spent more time on his own. He was really into music. Not just records and tapes but playing as well. He had a synthesizer in his bedroom. It was fixed so you could switch the sound to earphones, and Josh spent a lot of his spare time in this silent world of music.

Since Josh had had to give up sport at school he was working much harder, so the teachers let him get away with things that others couldn't have got away with. He was quite clever, and particularly good at languages.

However, there was a small but influential group of rude boys that didn't like Josh at all, and who started jostling him when they got the chance. Fortunately Josh was quite strong. I keep saying my little brother but he wasn't that little. I was tall. Josh was broad and beefy for his age.

In Josh's form the worst one was a boy known as Bag. How he got this name I don't know. Short for scumbag perhaps. Or sickbag. However he was quite frightening. Not to me or older blokes, of course, but to other 14-year-olds. Bag wanted to cause Josh trouble. He didn't know how successful he was going to be.

Before that comes another event. Josh and I were both in the school chess team. The games used to take place after school and on this occasion it was a home match. Josh and I were seated at opposite ends of a long table.

As soon as I saw Josh's opponent my blood ran cold. He had a horribly familiar colour and his white face contrasted with his red lips. I couldn't see his teeth but I didn't need to. He and Josh kept stealing glances at one another.

When, as usual, I'd nearly won and then lost by a silly mistake and so was free to move around, I paid the two of them a visit. Josh was quite good at chess but his game had gone to pieces under the pressure of this sudden increase in his circle of friends. I arrived just in time for checkmate. I didn't like the look of the victor at all. "This is David," said Josh. Dracula more like, I thought.

Dracula, as I will call him, clearly wanted to chat to Josh, and, equally clearly, did not want to talk in front of me. So I stuck to Josh like a limpet. That didn't help, for the damage was done. As the other team left, Dracula said to Josh, "We ought to see one another again. I'm sure we've got a lot in common. Here's my address." And he handed Josh a slip of paper.

Afterwards I thought of grabbing the paper from Josh. But what was the point? He knew where Dracula went to school, about fifteen miles away. More to the point Dracula knew where to find him. "He looked a nasty piece of work," I said to Josh. "Who?" he replied. "The pale bloke with the sharp teeth," I said. "Which one was that?" said Josh. I could see we were in for trouble.

It could have been worse. When Josh disappeared for the day the following Saturday, I thought it was going to be a great deal worse. Well, I couldn't be expected to guard him, could I? I'd spent the previous year or so trying to avoid him and I couldn't just turn round and become his inseparable companion. Anyway, Josh gave me the slip. He went down the road for an ice cream and got a bus instead.

Josh didn't return until ten o'clock that evening. By then Mum and Dad were anxious. I had to reassure them; not an easy thing since, if they were anxious, I was petrified. I told the truth. "He's gone to see a friend," I said. But not the whole truth. Well Dad, Josh has made friends with another vampire and they've gone to chew it over, if you know what I mean.

When Josh returned he looked normal enough. He hadn't got that look he gets after drinking the real stuff. So it didn't look as if he'd been gorging himself on young girls' blood or digging up graves or that sort of thing.

35

After we'd gone to bed Josh knocked on my bedroom
door and came and sat at the end of my bed.
"Well, how was your new friend?" I asked.
"I've learned a lot," said Josh.
And he told me what had happened.

CHAPTER 8

"David's family must be filthy rich," said Josh. "Loaded. Lots of dosh. You wouldn't believe the house. It's made of stone, with turrets and it looks like a castle. The only thing missing is a drawbridge."

"Was there a lot of mist?" I asked sarcastically, but Josh didn't get it.

"It's funny you should say that," he said, "because it was very misty there, sort of rising from the ground. There was a big pond in front of the house and I think it came from there."

"Don't tell me," I said. "You knocked on the door and a bloke with a big bolt through his neck opened it."

"No" said Josh. "It was David. Inside it was all panelled and David took me into a big gloomy room where I met his parents. They, were ...." he searched for words and in the end said " ......very like David."

I bet they were!

Josh continued, "They said they were very pleased to meet me and they looked forward to seeing a lot of me.

Meat's the word, I thought.

Then Josh said, "It's no use you looking disapproving Eg. After all, I'm a lot safer with them than you are. Vampires don't like other vampire's blood, it's like drinking your own blood."

"How do you know that?" I asked.

"David told me," said Josh. "He told me a lot."

He certainly had.   Apparently there were very few vampires around and they tried to keep it that way for fear of discovery.   It had seemed to Josh and I that if the thing was spread by blood contact then it could spread like wildfire.   You know what I mean. One bite and that's another vampire and then he goes out and has a bite and so on.

"Apparently it's not like that" said Josh.   "If you really bite hard, then once can be enough but otherwise it has no effect unless you do it again and again.   Then the person just gets weaker.   Then they go into a coma and seem to die.   Then they wake up as vampires."

"But how come they don't get discovered?" I asked. "I mean you can't go sucking pints of blood out of people and not expect them to complain or even notice."

Josh said, "The trick is to do it when they're asleep or at least when they're relaxed.   If you do it right it only leaves a little mark and there's something in the saliva that sends the person to sleep.   They think they dozed off and just had a bad dream."   I was thinking what sort of a lock I would put on my bedroom.

"And what about you?" I said to Josh.   "Who got at you?"
"My parents," he said.   "They were vampires.   It passes on to the children but only shows when they get into their teens."   And Josh told me the story of the gas explosion.

"David's parents know about it," he said. "They think the explosion was deliberate. They said to David that that's what happens if you go round biting the wrong people. At first they were worried I might be a bad influence on David."

The cheek of it, I thought. That David Dracula was a bad lot if ever I saw one.

Josh continued, "He's a really good guy. A bit wild but a lot of fun when you get to know him."

And that, I thought, was something I was definitely not going to do.

CHAPTER 9

For a week or two Josh and I went our separate ways. I had my life to lead didn't I. And I had Saffron.

Saffron was all the words I can't think of but which are at the tip of the tongue. She made my breath heave and my stomach go wobbly. She was wonderful and what was even more amazing was she liked me. Me. Eg. Spotty old Eg. I was in heaven.

Now you may remember my mentioning my girlfriend Susan. That relationship had been put under a lot of strain by this Josh thing. "You don't need a girlfriend, you've got your wretched brother," she said to me one day, and that was that.

Susan went round school announcing her new freedom. I kept my head down. Although down, my head turned when someone sat beside me on the bus going home from school. The someone was Saffron. Blonde, beautiful, in and out in all the right places. I cleared my throat and tried to think of something good to say. Nothing came except to ask if she had any hobbies. I didn't think that would impress her. In a state of blind panic I decided it was best to say nothing.

Then she said, "I hear you dumped Susan." That certainly wasn't what Susan had told every girl in the school. I tried to reply but only a squeak came out. She said, "Have you seen the film at the Plaza?"

Even I could get through the expected conversation to follow that. And so to the Plaza we went.

Saffron came round sometimes, even for a meal after I had carefully checked the menu. But most of the time I went round to her house. So I got a bit out of touch with Josh's comings and goings. We did go off to school together most mornings and I'd see him before I went out in the evening, usually to do my homework at Saffron's.

One evening I bumped into Josh as we both returned home at the same time. I noticed he had a reddish brown spot on the front of his shirt. He saw me look at it under the porch light as we stood by the front door. "We went to MacDonalds tonight," he said. "It's only tomato ketchup, don't worry". But I did worry. He had a look about him that hadn't come from eating a quarter pounder and fries.

Anyway, I forgot about that, or rather I made myself forget about it. What could I do? So long as Josh followed the rules he wouldn't hurt anyone or himself. That's what I said to myself.

In the meantime I had Saffron. And Saffron had a sister called Tabitha and I'd better tell you about her. Not, I hasten to add, because I fancied her or anything like that.

Tabitha was noisy and a bit naughty and she was in Josh's class. So the next thing could have been expected I suppose. You've seen films where the hero has escaped the monster, and locked and

41

bolted the house, and sits down to relax; and then it turns out the monster is in the kitchen. That's how I felt at Saffron's house when Tabitha turned up with Josh.

I got rid of Josh pretty quick. I told him Tabitha's living room had a big mirror in it and he found an excuse to leave. I knew I wasn't going to be able to put him off Tabitha. She was the fittest girl in his class and he wouldn't let her go in a hurry. Everyone was after her and that included the beastly Bag.

Josh was crazy about Tabitha. I will say one thing, it certainly made him get organised. It's a lot more difficult to avoid mirrors if you have a constant companion. Josh solved it by having Tabitha round our house as much as possible. So I didn't see much more of him. He'd be at home and I'd be at Saffron's.

Saffron didn't like Tabitha too much. I thought of my own troubles with Josh and I tried to make her feel better about her sister. "Tabitha's a really nice girl," I said, "and she's really popular and pretty." But that didn't seem to make things any better.

We were watching telly in Saffron's bedroom one evening after doing our homework when Saffron said, "Tabitha's not looking at all well lately. She looks all washed out, quite losing her looks."

I only got thinking about this when the commercial break came on. A nasty feeling started to come over me. I didn't go home early as I'd planned but waited for Tabitha to come. Josh brought her to the door. I got ready to go when I heard them arrive and all four of us stood in the hall. My heart sank as I saw the sore place at the base of Tabitha's neck. She fingered it several times, frowning slightly.

On the way home I had it out with Josh. In fact we nearly had a fight. "It's a mosquito bite," he said. I grabbed him by the collar.

"A 9 stone mosquito, you rat" I replied. Then Josh caved in. I think he was pleased to confess. "I've only done it twice, no three times," he said. "Look Eg I don't mean to. I can't help it. You know when we have a bit of a snog and she's so near and then I see that neck just there. Well, sometimes the teeth pop out and I just can't get them back in, if you know what I mean, and there you are." And there we were indeed.

"It's got to stop," I said. "You're weakening her. You've overdone it. What'll you do if she goes into a coma?

"I've got it under control," said Josh. "There's no danger." Famous last words I thought. I said, "I'm going to tell Dad." And I did.

CHAPTER 10

What had Dad been doing while all this was going on, and Mum? Well they went on and on at one another when they thought we weren't listening. First it was Dad. We heard him go on at Mum after we'd all gone to bed. That lasted several weeks. Then it seemed to be Mum's turn and it was her voice we'd hear.

Sometimes it seemed as if Josh and I didn't exist. After all, Josh was the problem but when we came in and they were talking they'd stop. I got a bit annoyed really. They'd been quite good at the beginning but now they now sort of took the problem away and made it private to them as if somehow that solved it. But it hadn't. They hadn't taken the problem away at all, and we were left with it without any help.

There was the occasional night when help did appear in the form of Mum or Dad or occasionally both of them waving a glass of whisky and wanting a heart to heart chat. I suppose that's all right if everyone in the conversation has been at it, but it didn't do a lot for me I must say. I'm glad I didn't know any of the dustmen. A good few empty bottles of whisky went into the bin that month.

Then Mum and Dad got to the stage where they wanted to talk. Well they'd missed their chance for a bit hadn't they. Saffron and Tabitha were on the scene and Josh and I had other worries and

44

thoughts on our minds: at least until Josh started using Tabitha as a drink dispenser.

So you can see that when the next day I said to Dad, "I say Dad I'm worried about Josh" he was pleased. Pleased to be told your son is drinking a young girl's blood! Well, every cloud has a silver lining.

"He's been at it with Tabitha, Dad," I said. Dad frowned and looked a bit puzzled. "With his teeth" I added.

"Oh my God!" said Dad. He walked round the room clutching his hair. He paced faster and faster. Any minute I expected him to start running round the room. Running round in circles was about it.

Then he spoke. "It's the only answer. I've discussed it with your mother. It's the only answer." Then he said, "I've got to get out of here for a bit. I'm going to the pub." Come on Eg, what a good chap you are, come along too and have a coca cola. Not on your life. I got a pat on the shoulder and "Thanks Eg, I'll talk to Mum and then we'll have a meeting." It's nice to be appreciated.

The meeting took place at tea time next day, which was a Saturday. We all sat round the table. I noticed Mum had developed a bit of a twitch in one eye. She looked very tired. She'd been very busy lately. It was near the end of term and she'd been out one evening a week on some course or other. Josh was quiet. Dad had ripped into him in the morning.

45

Dad plonked an old sports bag on the table. "Desperate times require desperate remedies," he said. He put his hand in the bag and fished around. Out came three business-like looking bottles, a long piece of rubber and a plastic case containing four syringes. You know, hypodermic syringes.

I thought of making a joke about whisky being preferable to drugs but I didn't because I could see at once what he was at. Mother's milk for baby Josh. Except it wouldn't just be from Mother, but Dad and guess who? Good old Eg. I felt a bit sad. I mean, it puts you in your place doesn't it when your main significance in the family is as a renewable source of eight pints of vampire plonk.

"We all have to do our bit," said Dad. "Mum, Eg and I will produce a safe amount of blood a week. You, Josh, will have a daily ration and an extra bit on Saturday evening. In return, Josh, you will not, I repeat not, however tempted, take blood from anyone else. That way no one else will get hurt, you won't get caught Josh, and you won't catch anything."

Dad must have had some idea how I felt for he hurriedly said, There's no need to worry Eg, Mum will do it for you. She's been on a first aid course so she'd know how to use the syringe and we've got books." Dad's concern was pleasing but he didn't know how I felt. If there's one thing that makes me close my eyes and shudder it's having a needle stuck in me. Silly isn't it. It doesn't hurt. I'd only really met this problem at the dentist's where it was overcome by the alternative of real pain. Even so, when I feel that needle going into my gums I think it's going to come out right through my chin. Ugh! And it seemed this was my reward for being brave.

Mum had a better idea of how I felt. She was looking at me and she said, "You don't have to do it darling. Dad and I can manage it. It's just that Dad, we, didn't want you to feel left out." Very thoughtful. Well Eg, we didn't want to miss you out so we decided to send you to the gas chamber too.

Later that evening Josh and I talked in my bedroom. "David's parents have done the same sort of thing," he said.

I replied, "But vampires don't like other vampires' blood."

"No" said Josh. "It's not quite the same. David's Dad is a doctor."

Heaven help us, I thought. I said, "Fancy going to your doctor. Hello Mrs. Smith, I think we'd better check up on your blood, glug, glug."

"No, not that sort of doctor," said Josh. He does research, studies blood. He's a sort of specialist, a private one." Very private I thought. This was secret drinking on a grand scale. "Anyway he can get as much blood as he wants for his work and he uses some of it to keep himself and his wife and David going." Josh frowned. "If you don't get any human blood at all, not even a tiny bit, you get ill. You don't die but you feel so awful in the end you just have to go and get some somehow."

"So that's why you and Dracula go out on Saturday nights together," I said. But Josh wasn't admitting anything.

"I've told you about Tabitha already, there isn't anything else," he said. "And now we're doing this I won't be tempted will I. And David and I haven't done anything wrong. We've got a lot in common to talk about. It's very lonely being a vampire you know."

Not half as lonely as being a vampire's brother, I can tell you.

CHAPTER 11

I daresay this arrangement could have gone on for years. Not for ever. After all, Josh would have to grow up and get married one day and then someone else would have to take over larder duty. Not an easy thing to explain on your wedding night, eh? I say, darling, here's a bottle. Could you just fill it up with blood?

It had gone on for about a month when trouble started, trouble that Josh solved in his own way. Josh was given a note by his form teacher to give to Mum and Dad. "The Headmaster and I," said the note," would like you to come and see us to discuss Josh."

What could it be? We tried to think what. "I've done nothing wrong," said Josh. "Not one bite and I've kept away from mirrors. All I do at school is work."

And that seemed to be the complaint! It's never happened to me and I bet it's never happened to you. I wasn't there, of course, but Mum and Dad kept going over it so I have it off by heart
"All he does at school is work" said his teacher.
"So what's wrong" says Dad.
"Well," said the teacher, "he's so white, and sometimes he seems very tired and he's lost all interest in sport."
Then the Headmaster comes into the conversation. "We're worried Josh is somewhat disturbed. He seems to have changed such a lot. I'm not saying

the change is bad but it's not normal. We think he should see a child psychiatrist."

"Blooming cheek," said Dad afterwards. "There's nothing wrong with Josh."

Who is kidding who, I thought. Still, it was good to feel Dad was on Josh's side, right or wrong.

"What could we say darling," said Mum to Josh. "They were only trying to help. We couldn't tell them to mind their own business, especially with me being a teacher."

So that was that. Mum and Dad signed Josh up to see the psychiatrist so as to keep the school happy, and Josh was told to go along with it. And so he did. You could say that he got his teeth into it.

The psychiatrist was a woman and Josh saw her at a clinic near the school. "She must be about thirty five," said Josh after the first visit. "But she doesn't look bad really, sort of cosy."

"What did she say?" I asked.

"Nothing" said Josh. "She just sort of sits there until I say something and then she lets me go on."

As my Dad says, if Josh fell down the lavatory he'd come up with a bar of chocolate. Just think of it. Let off school to see someone who's paid by someone else just to listen to you going on about yourself.

This went on for some weeks as Josh spilled all the family secrets bar one to his new friend. Then the psychiatrist told him there'd be only one more session.

"Well done, darling," said Mum.

"You've done a good job, old chap," said Dad.

50

More than you can say for the psychiatrist, I thought.

But was that the end of it? No, I'm afraid it wasn't. A final session the psychiatrist said. Just to help Josh on his way. That wasn't all he helped himself to

Josh told me about the final session. "I rambled on about Tabitha, and Mum and Dad. Then she asked me if I'd had any dreams this week. I shouldn't have said. Not really. Not at all. It was silly, but I told her I'd dreamed of being a vampire."

That's all we need. I thought. A public confession. Why not write to the papers?

Josh continued, "She laughed, and said I'd been watching too many DVDs. Then she said the session was at an end."

There was a long silence because I could see from the way Josh was looking that it wasn't the end. Then he said, "Well, I'd got to know her really well."
Actually, she'd got to know him really well (apart from the teeth, though Josh was to put that right). Josh didn't know anything about her at all.
"I wanted to say thank you," he said. He continued after a pause, "so I gave her a hug." There was an even longer silence and he said, "As I had my arms round her it was so near, her neck I mean."
We both lay on my bed, me looking at the ceiling and him at the floor.

Mum and Dad went round to the clinic the next day. They said they went to thank the psychiatrist, but actually they went to check up on what she was going to say about Josh to the school. They didn't stay long. Mum said the woman looked at them in a puzzled and sort of worried way while she kept touching this mark on her neck. They made a quick getaway. Dad gave Josh a right telling off afterwards.

CHAPTER 12

Our next half term was a week long. So was Mum's. Unusually, they coincided. Dad announced that we all needed a holiday and that he'd done a good business deal that would pay for it.

Dad booked the holiday as a surprise for all of us, including Mum, and was he pleased with himself. Now try and guess where we were going. I mean Josh didn't like daylight let alone the hot sun so it was obvious really. Iceland perhaps. Or possibly Norway. Somewhere cool with lots of trees and shade. You're right. He booked somewhere where we had guaranteed weather; sea, sand, sun and more sun.

Poor old Dad. He came in so pleased. We did try to be nice about it. Josh didn't say anything. Mum pointed out the problem. You had to laugh really. Anyway it was too late, it was all booked and paid for. Josh suggested Dad try to claim off the holiday insurance for the cost of cancelling it due to family sickness, meaning himself. Dad got quite stressy and said he was the one who was sick, sick of all of us, but he didn't mean it, at least I don't think so.

Was it hot when we got off the plane! Going through the door was like walking into a wall of heat. My heart sank . Everyone was in shirt sleeves and saying cor wot a scorcher and this is a bit of alright and so on, and there was Josh. I pretended I wasn't with him. He had dark glasses on, a wide brimmed hat and a long coat with the collar turned up. Mum was very good and kept chatting to him although he didn't reply. Dad looked distracted and was muttering to himself. His hair stood on end and he kept pulling it. At customs we all had to own up and stand together because Dad had the passports.

Dad cheered up a bit once we got past customs. That was because of the blood. What blood? A bottle full, Josh's supply for the holiday. Dad said he'd rather take a bottle of blood through customs than a syringe and I must say I agree.

We got a taxi to the villa. It was quite some way. Dad worked out that the taxi driver had cheated us on the fare. Unfortunately he only worked that out after he paid him and the man was driving off. Mum tried to jolly Dad out of it but I could see we were going to hear about this over the week.

I had a good holiday but it almost killed me. I liked the sun and swimming and I didn't want to miss that. But Josh understandably was a night bird. He kept to his bedroom in the day but at dusk he was up and ready to go. And why he shouldn't he. Goodbye Josh, see you later. Not likely. Mum and Dad said, "Whatever you do, don't let Josh out of your sight. You look after him Eg. We're relying on you. He can't go out in the day, but you've got to remember he's younger than you."

The first night Dad came with us, doing his bit. That wasn't a great success. After that we went out on our own. The village wasn't exactly packed with well known people but it suited Josh and me. To be more exact, it suited me until midnight and Josh until dawn.

What were our parents doing letting us out so late? I heard Dad say to Mum "I chose somewhere they'd like not somewhere we'd like. And it's a small place, isolated, but a good bit of night life. It's safe enough." Well, it was until Josh got there.

I have to say that from that point of view it was an absolute disaster. Every night it was the same. Off to the only disco that would let the likes of us in after midnight. Then Eg nods off about two a.m. He wakes up to see Josh, a Josh all lit up, in the air, full of you-know-what. I never saw the givers of these refreshments. Josh had got cunning about where he took a drink. Nor did I tell Mum and Dad. Every night, as dawn broke, I would return home with Josh: tired, and knowing that I had failed in my job, keeping his and my secret to myself.

There was a town about ten miles away from our little resort and on the third day Mum and Dad took themselves off there. Josh was in bed and I was sleeping by the pool when they returned. Dad was quite excited. "I hadn't thought of it," he kept saying. "What a chance." I grunted. Dad sat on the lounger beside me. "You can buy it Eg, actually buy it." I was exhausted after another evening of strenuous disaster but I managed another grunt. "Blood." said Dad. "You can buy blood, human blood, here."

I opened one eye. Then two. This was interesting. I sat up. Dad continued. "It's legal here. You can sell your blood and buy blood too. I'm going back tomorrow to find all about it."

And so he did. And the next day and the next. By night I had Josh, bopping and biting. And by day I had Dad going on about the blood business.

The next day Dad came back with a bottle of it and tried it out on Josh. It went down well. Josh sipped it like an expert. Well I suppose he was. He said it was slightly old but not bad at all.

The day before we left I found Dad pouring some of the stuff into a couple of wine bottles which he carefully sealed up. They looked just like ordinary bottles of wine. "That'll keep Josh going for a bit" said Dad. Would it? I wondered. How would Josh settle down to ordinary life after a week on the rampage.

It could have been worse. It nearly was. We sat in the plane in a line of five, Mum and Dad one side of the aisle and Josh and I and a woman on the other side. I bagged the window and Josh sat in the middle between me and this poor unsuspecting lady. Everything went well until we were half an hour from home and Josh's neighbour started to do herself up. First a hair brush. That was alright. Then a lipstick. Nothing much there. Then a compact. And in the compact? A mirror!

I didn't think anything of it until I felt Josh stiffen beside me. Then we both hunched back in our seats, squinting sideways. On went the lipstick.

Then she slapped her lips together in the mirror. Then a make-up pad. Then a long look in the mirror to make sure the whole set up was in order, a tilt to the left and then a tilt to the right.

She was about to put the compact away when she realised. She froze. Then, very slowly and casually, she undid the compact and looked at it, aiming the mirror at Josh. We know what she saw: herself, me and an empty place between us. She turned slowly, as if forcing herself and looked at Josh, then back and into her mirror.

One second she was there and the next she was gone. There was a spare seat at the other end of the plane and there she stayed. She'd left her bag under her seat and after landing as we made our way down the aisle to the door we passed her and she shrank away.

So much for her, I thought. But as we waited to collect our luggage I saw her in a corner watching us. Then as we moved towards customs I saw her talking to a policeman and pointing at us. I nudged Dad. He had seen what had happened on the plane. I heard him say, "Josh get the hell out of here." And Josh did, through the green customs channel with no luggage and his passport in one hand. Goodbye Josh.

And hello to one hysterical woman, a policeman and several customs officers. "Excuse me officer" I heard Dad say. "What's that? Can't be seen in a mirror? Is this some sort of joke?" By now the woman was in full flow and they didn't know what to do with her. One of the customs men went off and came back with a man in a white coat. He and the policeman then led the lady off. She was crying by now. I felt sorry for her but family has to come first. That's what Dad said. When we got through customs we found Josh in the cafeteria stuck into a huge milkshake.

CHAPTER 13

I suppose Josh would have told Dad about Dracula sometime. He certainly didn't expect Dracula to call, or he would have told him not to. It had to be Dad who went to the door didn't it.

We were having a meal in the kitchen. "Who can that be?" he said, and went to the front door. I heard it open and then a silence. Then the door slammed and Dad rushed into the kitchen. "My God, it's another one," he said.
"Another what, darling?" said Mum.
"Another ..... another .." said Dad pointing at Josh.
Mum's jaw dropped. So did the knife in her hand.
"Oh no," she said "not another one."
I agreed. One was enough, more than enough. To be precise, one more than enough.

Josh jumped up. "It must be David." He rushed out of the room and we heard the front door open.
"And who's David?" said Dad.
"He's a friend of Josh's," I said.
"And has he been like this for long?" asked Dad. "Has Josh been spreading it around? I hope you don't think I'm being nosy. I'd just like to know if your brother is chewing his way through the whole town."
"But ...," I said. That was all I got in.
"I know one when I see one" said Dad. He was right, and so did I. He continued, "Where does this friend come from then?"

I tried to make the best of it. "He's from a very respectable and old established vampire family."

"Great," said Dad. "Count Dracula I presume." Maybe he was right. I said nothing.

Josh came back into the kitchen. "I caught him up," he said, "and I've put him in my room. You'll like him. He's a really good bloke."

"Right young man," said Dad. "We've got a few questions for you."

Josh explained how he'd met David. "And what about his family?" said Dad. "I suppose they live in a castle with turrets and panelling."

"How did you know?" said Josh.

"This is all we need," said Dad.

"His Dad is very posh," said Josh. "He's a doctor."

"A doctor!" shouted Dad. "A doctor! Why don't you tell me he's an alcoholic who runs an off-licence." This was familiar, I thought. Still, I'd better put Dad right.

I said, "He's not a family doctor Dad, he specialises in blood, studies it, that's how he gets supplies for himself and his family."

Dad calmed down a bit. "Alright for some," he said.

Mum said, "Why doesn't Josh ask David down."

"I call him Dracula," I said, but Dad was deep in thought and ignored me.

He said to Josh, "This chap knows all about blood then?" Josh nodded, and Dad continued, "He'd know how long it keeps, and how you check if it's infected and so on?"

Josh said, "I suppose so."

Dad beamed and slapped him on the back. "Well Josh, old chap, bring your little friend down and let's meet him."

I'm sure you've realised what Dad was about. It took me a few minutes to put two and two together. Dad had put them together. Blood and business that's what they were. And free drinks for life for Josh.

So it was that several days later I found myself in our car outside Dracula's house. I think Dad had felt rotten about what he'd said to me. Anyway, he'd asked me to come with him. Only in the car mind. The guilt didn't extend to inviting me in with him. That was for grown ups only.

The front door closed. It was a fine day and I thought I'd walk round the garden. As I turned the corner of the house heading for a huge lawn I saw an open window. It was hung with thick curtains but I heard voices.

"I thought I should come and see you for Josh's sake," I heard Dad say. "And because I think we may have something to offer one another." There was a silence. Dad continued. He explained how we were coping with Josh's need for human blood. Then he told Dracula's father, Big Drac I'll call him, about the holiday and the blood. And he spoke of his worries about infected blood and the dangers of Josh catching something. Then he said, "I'm told you're an expert on blood. Well, I'm a businessman and I know about buying and selling, and importing and exporting. Between us we know everything that's

61

needed to make a business of this and have a good surplus of blood over into the bargain."

After that there was a lot of business stuff. Interesting if you like that sort of thing. Then my ears pricked up. Big Drac said, "I'm very pleased you've come. I was worried that Josh would be a bad influence on David."

Wow! I waited for the explosion but Dad said, "And I was worried about David being a bad influence on Josh. We have a lot in common, haven't we?" What rats these grown ups are.

I decided it was time I stopped listening but Dad changed the conversation and said, "So, Josh inherited his condition. I understand you know something about his history and his parents."

Big Drac sighed. He sounded as if he had the cares of the world on his shoulders. I know the feeling. I heard a sort of hiss, a kind of long and tired breathing out. He said, "I knew them, I knew his father when he was a child. A group of us moved to this country at the same time years ago. In the old land he was always a wayward boy, there was no controlling him. We had hoped marriage would quieten him down." There was a silence and he said, "He caused a lot of trouble. You know, we live by secrecy, keeping to ourselves. We can't afford to have someone wreck it all. He was wild, created new members of the family without thought. He had to be stopped he could have wrecked our new lives." Family! This was all going too fast for me.

Big Drac said, "We were going to deal with it. But someone else got there before us. That's how it would be if the likes of him did what they wanted. We'd all be condemned."

Dad said, "You were boys together?"

Big Drac laughed. It didn't sound nice. I hoped I'd see Dad again. Big Drac said, "Not exactly. Josh's father's father and I went to school together." Well, that's long life for you. It's not all it's cracked up to be.

Then it was if Big Drac had shaken himself like a dog and thrown something off him. His voice changed. It was weird. Suddenly it all sounded so normal. "You must all come and see us," he said. "Isn't that so darling?" I realised Mrs. Drac must have been there beside him while he and Dad talked.

"That's very kind of you" said Dad.

Mrs Drac spoke, "We're having some friends round next Sunday," she said. "For drinks at twelve o'clock. Do bring Josh. And your other son." She added, "That's 12 midnight, of course."

It was time to go. I swiftly ran round the corner of the house and got in the car.

CHAPTER 14

Drinks at the Dracs! "What shall I wear?" said Mum. "How about a shroud?" I replied, but she wasn't

63

listening. I wasn't too worried about what to wear myself. I wasn't planning to pull some nice young vampire.

I told Josh what I'd overheard. He looked very thoughtful. "Are you related to the Dracs then?" I asked.

"No" he replied. "They refer to all vampires as the family. David's real family were the posh lot unlike my parents. It seems we came from the same place, probably running away from whoever was after us." I wasn't too keen on the "us" bit. I know which side I'd have been on.

Big Drac opened the door, a glass in one hand. He was tall with a high forehead and black hair; very distinguished in a corpselike sort of way. Dad did the introductions. When it came to my turn Big Drac shook me by the hand. "Hello Egbert," he said. "You're the one who looks after Josh." He'd got the picture. I began to think he might not be so bad after all.

Josh vanished with Little Drac and I was left standing in a corner of the room. I will say it was luxurious in a creepy sort of way. A crystal chandelier hung over a deep red thick carpet. That's not all it hung over. Underneath was a room full of vampires. There were about twenty of them, short and tall, thin and fat, young and old. And very old and even older, I thought.

Someone caught me by the arm. I started and looked round. It was a short and apparently middle-aged woman in a billowing dress that looked as if it hid rolls of fat. She had lipstick across her face. The lipstick was shaped in a revolting smile. I don't know what she was smiling at. She fingered my arm. Perhaps she was feeling how tender I'd be. I watched to see if she licked her lips.

But she didn't. She said, "You must be the new boy's brother. She squinted at me. "You're name's Ogg, isn't it?"
"Eg," I said.
"I knew it was a funny name." She went on, "You remind me of my son Herman." I felt sorry for Herman.

The smile got wider. She wobbled. She said, "I married into the family you know. It was a mixed marriage. I used to give my little boy his drinky every Saturday." She had a scarf round her throat and she pulled it down. I could see lots of little scars. Yuck, I thought. I'm all for mother love but this was revolting. She went on, "When Herman stated work I converted. You know what I mean." I knew alright. I hoped she had a good supply of the hard stuff tucked away somewhere and didn't have her eye on me for cocktails.

"There's Herman," she said. Herman looked a fat thirty five. She pulled my arm, "He's got a good job, you know". In a mortuary no doubt, I thought. "He's a funeral director," she said.

65

That was it. I'd had enough but I couldn't get rid of her. I could see no one else wanted to talk to her and she wasn't going to let an audience go that easily. Then she said, "It's not easy having one of us in your family when you're not all like it. I know. You lead your own life Ogg. Make your own friends." She patted me on the shoulder. "Now you don't want to be talking to me all night, do you."

She was dead right. Off I went to find the loo. On my way back I was about to enter the hall when I heard voices on the other side of the door.

One said, "They seem all right. Safe enough. The parents seem to have it surprisingly well under control. I don't think we'll have to do anything."
Then I heard Big Drac's voice say, "The boy's wild. He worries me."
The first voice said, "The rest of his family will keep him in check."
"I hope you're right," said Big Drac. "That brother of his may help. But the parents can only control what they know about." Then he said, "The father has got some interesting business ideas."

I crept down the passage back to the loo, and then walked noisily back to the door and pushed it open. Big Drac was standing at the front door saying goodbye to a strong looking man, short with wide shoulders and a black moustache and beard. They both looked at me as I walked by and into the room full of guests.

It wasn't so full now. Mum and Dad were ready to go. I could tell from the way they stood. "Go and get Josh, darling" said Mum. But as I turned, Josh and Little Drac came into the room. Little Drac nudged Josh and pointed to a man sitting in a chair. Sprawling was the word really. He was lying back with a vague look and a big silly smile on his face.

Herman and his mother passed us on their way out. She held me by the arm. "You look after your mother Ogg, and keep an eye on that brother of yours." She looked at the smiling man. He was hiccupping gently from time to time. "Disgusting," she said. "Dreadful manners. He must have drunk it before he came. I don't know where he gets it from." She squeezed my arm. "Don't think we're all like that my dear."

As we drove home Mum said, "Well that was nice, wasn't it darlings. It was good to have a chance to look them over." Dad grunted. I agreed. Who was looking who over? Not much doubt about that.

Mum continued, "They seem very nice really, polite and friendly and well behaved. Even that one who had a drop too much was very quiet about it." A drop too much of what, I thought.

Josh said, "They were really angry with him. It's the height of bad manners with them."
"Getting drunk?" said Mum.
"No," said Josh. "Bingeing on blood."
That was a conversation stopper. Mum said, "Oh," and went very quiet. Dad said nothing but I noticed

we were doing fifty-five in a thirty-mile-per-hour speed limit.

Josh seemed pleased with the effect. He said, "That's what happens if you have too much. It's like getting drunk. Not that I know what that's like." Huh, who was he kidding? "You feel really happy, you wouldn't argue with anyone" he added.

I think Josh was expecting us all to be asking him questions about it with him as the centre of attention. I could see Mum and Dad were really depressed though. Josh said, "It's very bad manners to do it in public, you see. Blood is scarce and it's a waste and a sort of showing off." Josh knew all about that.

By the time we were out of the speed limit Dad had slowed down a bit. He said, "David's father's a clever man, and friendly enough, but he makes me feel uneasy."

I thought of repeating what I'd heard. "I don't think we'll have to do anything," the bearded man had said. Do anything? Do what? There are some things it's best not to think about. We were going quite fast enough for me and I decided to say nothing.

CHAPTER 15

This little outing seemed to produce a general relaxation. We all felt relieved in some way. I think it was Mum's turn to feel that a trouble shared was a trouble halved. Dad for some reason felt confident in Big Drac. In fact, from time to time, he'd pop over and see him. "Strictly business, Eg," he'd say. "Look, no bites." Josh felt approved of. I was going to say he felt less of a freak but that would have been wrong. Josh didn't appreciate how much of a freak he was.

And what about poor old Eg I hear you ask. Well for once poor old Eg didn't feel too bad. In fact it was going good for me. I was beginning to feel free of Josh. I still had plenty to do with him but I didn't feel he was my responsibility the way I did before. And I had Saffron, beautiful, wonderful, super-cool Saffron. Even my spots had started to clear up.

What was funny was that just as I was getting rid of the burden of brother Josh I started to be rewarded for bearing it. "I don't know what we'd have done without you, Eg," Dad would say as he pushed a crisp note into my top pocket. "Here, you deserve a bit of a treat, darling," Mum would say as she pressed another into my hand. When I remembered, I tried not to look too happy, in case this flood of appreciation might end.

And I suppose I got used to the situation. That made it easier. When Saffron said, "What's the matter with Josh? He's really nice and he's cool but sometimes he makes me feel really creepy," did I turn a hair? Not at all. "There's nothing wrong with my brother," I said. "He's just a full blooded Englishman." Full of blood. That was right. Not all his own unfortunately.

And so we might have all lived happily ever after. Well for a while anyway. But. That's the word. But what? But Bag, that's what.

Now we have got to this point I had better tell you about the Bag family. Bag was the tip of an iceberg. The biggest and worst bits were out of sight, at home.

Bag's surname was Scurf, an appropriate name if ever there was one. Even worse than being called Eg. Mrs Scurf was a huge woman, smelly, with long black greasy hair and filthy fingernails. Bag's family called her Ma and they were afraid of her. Just as well. They weren't afraid of anyone else, that's for sure.

"They" were Bag's father, Bag's two older brothers and his sister. The brothers were Charlie and Freddie, a right couple of layabouts who collected unemployment benefit and did odd jobs. "Work shy", the teachers called them when they lectured Bag on not getting like the rest of his family. Bag couldn't wait!

Bag's brothers had greasy hair as well because of all the stuff they put on it. They were a nasty pair who liked to fight and they'd both been up in Court for that sort of thing.

Their sister's hair wasn't greasy, it was blonde. Well, sort of yellow, like straw, except sometimes her parting was black. "That's a real dirty girl," Dad said once. But she always looked very clean to me. Saffron didn't like her at all, nor did any of the girls. Sandra, that was her name, had left school the year before. She worked in a shop and went out with older men. I wouldn't have wanted to go out with her myself, of course, but I could see what they saw in her. And at least she had a job; that's what Mum and Dad said.

Mr Scurf was a thin man with a moustache and a face like a ferret. He often had a ciggie stuck to his lower lip. He talked very quietly in an undertone as if what he was saying was a secret. I daresay a lot of it was. Mr Scurf did "deals". Not big deals but little ones, mostly to do with old cars. The remains of this business littered the Scurfs' backyard and their front garden and the drive at the side and the road leading to their house. The Scurfs were not good neighbours to have.

As a family the Scurfs were very close. They were bound together even more by their love of music. By that I don't mean they sat down in the evenings listening to Beethoven. No, the Scurfs idea of a good evening was playing heavy rock. And when I say playing I don't mean putting on a CD. I mean they belted it out themselves. The line up was Freddie on the saxophone, Charlie on the bass and Pa and Bag on guitars. In front was Sandra doing her vocals and behind the family, as ever, was Ma, on the drums.

Bag was the baby of the family, if that's the right way to describe a musical thug. He could just about read and write which was more than Pa could, although Pa could count, no doubt about that, especially fifty pound notes.

Actually, Bag was artistic as well as musical. He definitely had a gift. He couldn't stop doing it, and you could see Bag's artistry everywhere, on bus shelters, buses, walls, posters, anywhere that a spray can and Bag's arm could reach. Yes, Bag was a graffiti artist. He was just like Van Gogh really, unrecognised in his time.

That isn't strictly true, because every so often Bag would be recognised and it got him into a lot of trouble I'm pleased to say.

The Scurfs were a bit like an illness or a natural disaster. You avoided them if you could but if you came into contact with them you weren't surprised when your life took a downwards turn for a bit. And avoid them I did, but for Josh it wasn't so easy. One reason was that Bag was in the same year. The second reason was that Bag was mad about Tabitha. And that really was a problem, a big problem.

The fateful day was hot and sunny, not something to put Josh in a good temper. He had every inch of shade at school well mapped. At the side of the school was a thicket of evergreen trees. As we got off the bus Josh, collar up and shades on said, "I'm going to meet Tabitha before lunch under the trees, why don't you come too? I'll see you at the clearing." Very social. Josh wanted to mix his pleasures, chat to me and see Tabitha while he had a secret smoke.

So, at lunch time I hurried to the clearing. I was late. Unfortunately so was Josh. It was Tabitha who had got there first. And who came second? Not Josh but Bag, sneaky big horrible Bag, trailing Tabitha and with naughty thoughts in his head.

I have to say that Tabitha didn't object to boys eyeing her up. Bag was pretty gross but he pulled the birds. Sometimes I felt Tabitha could have told him to get lost a little more firmly. Anyway Bag clearly thought he was in with a chance and Tabitha got a nasty surprise.

So when Josh came into the clearing it was to see Bag struggling with Tabitha and trying to kiss her. As Josh said later, "I'm afraid I just lost my temper Eg, but wouldn't you?" I jumped on him. He threw me off, and I gave him one on the nose."

That was when I arrived. Tabitha faced me crying. On my left was Bag; big, brawny and very angry. And from Bag's smacked nose dripped, yes you've got it, blood. On my right was Josh, breathing heavily, shades thrown on the ground, shaking with anger. But in his eye was the look I knew only too well and his nostrils flared.

73

This particular beefsteak was tough, however. Josh was strong. He'd kept fit by jogging. Yes, at night. There's many a true word spoken in jest and Josh was in pretty good condition what with that and a high protein vampire diet. But Bag was stronger and as they grappled it was clear that Josh was in difficulties.

Yes, I know. I should have defended my little brother. I should have helped him. Instead, he helped himself, so to speak.

As they struggled, Josh's face came near to Bag's bloodstained face. I could see the look in Josh's eye. Thinking of your next meal doesn't improve your performance in a fight. Then Bag broke Josh's grip, pushed him away and landed him a dreadful thump on the cheek. Josh went down and Bag went after him. Josh was on his back now with Bag sitting on top. Josh held Bag's arms off but slowly Bag forced his hands down.

Tabitha screamed and I realised I should be helping. But as I stepped forward it happened. The fateful deed I mean. Instead of pushing Bag's arms away Josh suddenly pulled one towards him and sank his teeth into it.

The effect on Bag was extraordinary. He went out like a light. He just collapsed on top of Josh. I rushed to pull Bag off and as I dragged him from Josh I found he and Josh were firmly attached to one another by Josh's teeth. Josh's eyes were closed and his jaw was clenched and his Adam's apple bobbed up and down as he swallowed. I moved quickly so Tabitha couldn't see this feeding time at the zoo. With great difficulty I forced Josh's jaws open and pulled him away. He and Bag lay on their backs breathing heavily. I leant over Josh. "For goodness sake get your teeth back in or Tabitha will see," I said.

"Oh no, what have I done?" Josh said. His words were a bit muffled because he had his hand over his mouth. Next, Tabitha was all over him, crying, and saying how proud she was of him. Then Bag came round with a jerk, as if he'd started out of a deep sleep. He was on his feet in a moment, crouching and ready to fight.
"The fight's over Bag" I said. "You passed out. You ought to see a doctor."
Bag rubbed his eyes blearily. He straightened up. There was a puzzled look about him. Not surprising. By the way, Bag, you've just been bloodsucked by a vampire.
"Honest," I said. "That's right, isn't it, Tabitha?" And Tabitha said that was right.
Bag shook his head. Then he noticed his wrist and rubbed it. He looked at Josh. "You watch it you stuck up git, I'll get you," he said. And he shambled off. And so did we. We went to lunch although Josh had already had his.

That evening Josh said to me "I'm worried Eg. I absolutely lost my temper. The way I bit him, I've never done that to anyone."

"Don't worry," I said. Being Josh he didn't. And being me I did. With good reason.

CHAPTER 16

We soon had plenty to take our minds off the awful Bag. Term ended in a couple of days and we were off on holiday again. Again was the word. Back to the land of sea, sun and blood supermarkets. We took our own company with us. Who would you vote holiday companions of the year, real fun to be with, a laugh a minute? Yes, that's it. We went with the Dracs.

The holiday was a complete surprise to Josh and me. Dad announced it the day after Josh bit Bag. "Vladimir and I have an interesting business idea which we want to investigate further while we're all on holiday. We thought it would be nice if both families came." I didn't know why he was being so mysterious. We all knew what it was about.

"Are we going to stay in that apartment again" said Josh, making a face. Josh would have preferred a cellar or perhaps a nice deep hole in the ground. Dad said, "Well, you won't believe the coincidence but Vladimir apparently has a family home there. It's on the edge of the main town."

It was not surprising that Vladimir, Big Drac to you and me, arranged for us to go on a night flight. "It's much cheaper," Mum said. "And Josh will be better travelling at night." What about Eg, I thought.

Big Drac was quite right though. On a night flight we were normal and inconspicuous. There was no need to hide from the sun. We arrived at dawn. Outside the airport building I looked for the cab rank but Big Drac led the way to a pair of new Mercedes cars with darkened windows. The drivers stood by the open doors bowing and scraping. I looked on the Dracs with new eyes and steeled myself to learn how the other half lived. After all, one has to be prepared to make sacrifices.

From the airport we drove to the town and through its empty streets to the other side. We turned into a drive passing through old iron gates set in a high stone wall which seemed to stretch endlessly either side. I noticed someone had painted graffiti over it.

Down the drive we went, past silent heavy leaved ancient trees until we scrunched to a stop in front of the house. It sat there looking at us blindly, its two storeys of shuttered eyes closed. As I got out of the car it was the silence that struck me. No noise, no birds, even the leaves didn't seem to rustle. It was as if everything was holding its breath.

That was broken by Mum and Dad doing their "isn't it lovely" bit. "A fine building," said Dad. "Do you visit here often?"
"I haven't been here for some years" said Big Drac.
Just then the front door opened and out came an old man. He looked strong but bent. I thought he must be the caretaker. I will say Big Drac was very attentive to him and put his arm round his shoulder while they talked in some strange language.

It was certainly a different holiday but I can't say I liked it. Quite sensibly, those of the vampire variety went on to night shift, getting up at the end of the afternoon and going to bed in the morning.

Sometimes Big Drac would stay up and go off with Dad on business. Mum sunbathed and went shopping. As for Josh and Little Drac, I didn't know what they did and I didn't want to. I, Eg, was left, as they say, to my own devices for most of the day.

The house seemed deserted, full of large, high-ceilinged rooms cool with marble floors. I could go where I wanted except for one door which led to a separate part of the house and which was kept locked. I saw Big Drac go there several times and once I saw the caretaker come out. I decided that that must be where he lived.

Please don't think I went everywhere else. Not to the Dracs' bedroom for sure. And certainly not to the cellars. What was down there, I wondered. Rows of open coffins perhaps.

Nor did I go to the servants' quarters at the back, where the two chauffeurs lived. They did everything. One doubled up as a cook and one as a butler. They both cleaned the house and did the gardening. I'd say they worked from dawn 'till dusk but that wouldn't be correct. They worked from dusk until dawn (and a bit after). They didn't like the sun if you know what I mean.

You will not be surprised that I found all this really boring. I went out with Little Drac and Josh one night but not again. One vampire perhaps, two definitely not. I felt outnumbered.

Actually we didn't have a repeat of Josh's performance last time, or not initially. Big Drac saw to that. He had them into his room and gave them a right warning. "Very frightening," said Josh. That might not have been enough, for Josh wasn't one to stay frightened for very long. But Big Drac had one of the servants follow them round to make sure they got up to no good. He also insisted that they came back by two o'clock. Little Drac didn't mind but Josh didn't think much of it. "Back by two o'clock!" he said. "It's ridiculous. It's like saying you can't go out in the afternoon." He complained of being bored. Once he woke me up in the middle of the night, but only once. After that I locked my room; probably a sensible precaution anyway.

One afternoon I was reading in the ballroom. Yes there was even a ballroom on one side of the house. And I was reading because that was all there was to do in the hot afternoon. There was no TV and not even a radio. I had my walkman on while I was reading. Looking at my watch I saw it was five o'clock. Teatime. Or breakfast time, according to your taste. I headed for the kitchen. On my way I passed the caretaker's door. It was open.

I was tempted by the door. Resisting temptation has never been my strong point. I sneaked through the door, down a short corridor and into a room. What a

80

room! It was huge. One long wall was covered in books. Not just any old books but really old books, beautiful books, bound in leather with gold lettering on them. On the other walls were paintings. It was like an art gallery. I thought I remembered one of the paintings from an art book I'd read.

I was looking at the furniture, which was like something out of a museum, when I heard the voice. "Good evening young man. I wondered when you would pay me a visit." The voice was really posh. What my Dad would call an Oxford accent.

I looked round. At first I thought there was no one there. Then I saw a high backed leather chair in a corner. And in the leather chair I saw the caretaker. It can't be him I thought and continued looking. "Yes, it's the caretaker," said the voice. "Come over here my dear chap."

I couldn't tell how old he was although I knew he must be old, really old. He had the vampire look but his face was almost weather-beaten. He had the hint of a smile at the edges of his mouth and a twinkle in his eye. "Well young man" he said. "Welcome to the vampire's den. Can I offer you a cup of tea and a piece of cake perhaps?"

I wasn't sure what I should say to this. I thought of saying, "Thank you. I haven't had a bite all day" but that didn't seem a good idea. So I smiled and nodded instead. He rang the bell and one of the servants came in. He bowed to the old fellow who said, "Boris, some cake for the young gentleman." I'd never heard the servant, Boris, speak English before. He said, "Certainly my lord," all posh, a real classy accent just like a butler in a film.

It was beginning to occur to me that this old bloke wasn't the caretaker. "I'm Vladimir's father" he said. He added "Boris speaks seven languages but he likes to keep himself to himself." He poured a cup of tea and passed it to me. "I speak twelve languages. We have had plenty of time to learn them in."

His lordship, as I will call him, sipped his tea. "It is a pleasant country here, is it not?" he said. Since I didn't agree with him I said nothing. "You don't agree," he said. "I'm not surprised. This must be a boring holiday for you. We'll have to see what we can do." He took another sip. "I have got used to it here, it is beginning to be home for me."

I thought I had better make an effort so I said, "Where are you from?"

"An ungrateful land," he said. "We had lived there for many years. Then we and ours, our family, you know what I mean by 'family', had to leave. Vladimir and a number of others, including your brother's parents, eventually found themselves in your country." He looked sad. "I had lived and studied in many countries but always I returned home. Maybe I will again one day. But this house had belonged to my family for many years and I came here in the end. This is my home now. Have some cake." And he handed me a plate Boris had brought in while he was talking.

I felt a bit sorry for him. Once you get to know these vampires you can see they are a bit sad and depressed. "There's not a lot to do here," I said. "Do you have any friends living nearby?" I felt I wasn't doing well. I added, "I suppose you do most of your socialising at night." I felt I was doing worse.

But his lordship laughed. "There's not a lot of that, but we do go out at night, and dusk and dawn. We're used to living here, and there's the blood, and my books." He waved at them. "I study," he said.

I was busy nodding and trying to look interested when he said, "I've got earphones too. What have you been listening to?" I told him.

I was really amazed when he said, "That's not bad but I prefer "Guns & Roses." I only realised how long we'd been talking about music when I saw I'd eaten the whole plate full of cakes.

"How do you know all this?" I said. "I haven't heard any music, and there's no T.V. or radio in the house."
"The family wouldn't like it" he said. "It would upset Boris and Levin as well." Levin was the other servant. "They've been with me for two hundred years. I'd feel I was letting them down. One has to fulfil one's role."

One certainly has, I thought. I waited and said nothing. He said, "I listen to the radio with my earphones in bed."

83

There was a knock on the door. "Here," I said. "Keep this". I thrust the CD from my MP3 player into his hands. I also took one of Josh's heavy rock CDs from my pocket and gave it to him. I heard the door open as his lordship stuffed his hand deep into the wide pocket of his silk dressing gown.

Big Drac strode into the room. "Good evening father, did you sleep well?" Then he saw me. That put him off his stroke. I know something you don't know, I thought.

I stayed up late that night talking to Josh. That pleased him and I got more out of him than usual. Josh was beginning to get very secretive about his long-toothed friends. But not tonight, although he was a bit awkward at first.
"Why didn't you tell me the caretaker was Big Drac's father," I said to Josh.
"You didn't ask," he said.
"You might have told Dad and Mum," I said.
"It's none of their business," said Josh. Which family do you belong to, I thought.

But Josh couldn't resist the chance to tell a good story once the news was out. "His lordship seems a really nice bloke," he said. "But he used to be very fierce. He lived in a big castle and terrorised everyone for miles around. But eventually the neighbouring Barons got together and drove him out. They burned the castle down and chased round with sharpened stakes and so on. His lordship and his relations and friends and servants escaped just in time."

"He didn't do too badly out of it," I said.

Josh nodded his head vigorously. "David said they took five wagon-loads of gold and jewellery with them. Hundreds of years of plunder."

"How did they get here, and to home?" I asked, meaning our home.

Josh told me. "His lordship travelled, all over Europe and beyond, and some of them went with him. Vladimir was very young then and they had a nanny look after him because his mother had died. The people who looked after him, and some of the others, moved to another country and settled there. His lordship used to visit them but in the end he finally settled here. David said his father said he came here just to show how bloody-minded he was. Anyway, then something went wrong with Vladimir's lot and they had to move again in a hurry. That was when Vladimir had grown up, a lot later. David says he thinks he, David, had an older brother who was killed. I think somehow they got found out and they were attacked. That was when they moved to our country but they had trouble there too. That's when my parents were killed. Then Vladimir and some of his friends moved again to where we live.

"That was a coincidence," I said.

Josh replied, "Yes, I suppose it was. Maybe it wasn't a coincidence. I was adopted after they moved here. I know they kept an eye on me." I bet they did.

"I don't think we'll have to do anything," the bearded man had said.

CHAPTER 17

I went on to the night shift. If you can't beat them join them. Well, join them a bit. Not all the way if you know what I mean. It worked really well. It didn't mean going to bed all day, just from about ten or eleven in the morning to four or five in the afternoon. So I still saw plenty of Mum and Dad.

"Not joining the opposition?" Dad asked. He said it like a joke, but I knew he was anxious.
I put his mind at rest. "Only mosquito bites Dad," I said. Actually it didn't put his mind at rest. When I was sunbathing I saw him looking for bites.

Dad said to me, "Did you know the caretaker was Vladimir's father".
"Yes," I said. I could see Josh had spread the word now he knew it was out.
"Why didn't you tell me, ratface" said Dad.
"You didn't ask me," I said.

Poor old Dad. Poor old Mum really. Dad was busy, rushing around, with and without Big Drac, seeing officials, talking about blood and phoning and phoning on his mobile. God knows what the calls cost.

At first I thought there wasn't a phone in the house but there was. I suppose Big Drac and his lordship wanted to keep in touch. It was kept in a box in a room off the entrance hall. The box was usually kept locked but with all this use they left it open sometimes. I popped in and made a note of the number. I like to know where I am and I thought it might come in useful. It did.

Later, I said to his lordship, " I see you have a phone."
"I can't keep up with these modern things," he said. " That's why we keep it locked up".
" What about the internet," I said.
"I've never been attracted to fishing," he replied.

We talked a lot about music. I said to him, "You need to get a proper sound system, that kit and earphones are no good at all. You can't even play those CDs I gave you."
"Oh, I couldn't do that, my dear chap" he said.
"It's your house," I said. "You should do what you want in it.
"Vladimir wouldn't like it," he said.
"Then he'll have to lump it," I said.
He was thinking deeply, a little smile crawling over his lips. "Alright," he said. "You can take me shopping."

The shops were open in the evenings and that's when we went out. I waited in the hall for his lordship. I couldn't believe it when he arrived. He wore a wing collar and tails.

His lordship drove the Mercedes. The streets grew narrow as we got to the old quarter of the town. We drew up outside a big old shop. "They should have what we want here," he said. I noticed we'd parked in a no parking area but it didn't seem to worry his lordship.

There was a young assistant behind the counter. As I closed the door behind us he looked up. Then he did a double take. His eyes boggled. A sort of squeak came out of him and he dashed out through a door at the back.

His lordship took no notice and wandered round the shop looking at equipment. I heard a nervous cough and turned round. There stood an elderly man, evidently the shop owner, his hands together in a moving handshake with himself. I could have sworn he shook. He spoke to my lord in the language of the land. "My good man," said his lordship, and very lordly with it too. "Please speak in English so my young friend can understand.

There were a lot of "sirs", and "your honours" and "my lords", before the deal was done. You certainly wouldn't have mistaken him for a caretaker. "My man will pay you tomorrow" he said and out we swept, with the owner carrying the goods to the car. He called for his assistant but the young man didn't appear.

As we got to the car I could see a policeman was about to put a parking ticket on it. But as he saw his lordship bear down on him he went white, stuffed the ticket in his pocket, and hurried off in the opposite direction crossing himself.

We had great fun when we got back, setting it up. Then we put it on, full volume.

Big Drac was the first to arrive. He charged in. I was adjusting the balance while his lordship sat in his high-sided leather chair. Big Drac was in a real mood. "How dare you make this row in my father's room!" he shouted. "Don't you have any respect at all, you and your brother?"

I turned the sound down. Out of the leather chair came the voice, long and clear like a bell, like a hatchet more like. "Vladimir, this is my noise, my son, and it pleases me. My friend Egbert is full of respect. Aren't you Egbert."
I buried my face in the music centre. Quarrels between old-age pensioners were none of my affair.
"Have you gone mad, father?" said Big Drac.
"No," he said. "I'm just pleasing myself with what is mine. Turn it up Egbert." And I did. And Big Drac left. He wasn't happy. Not happy at all.

Boris didn't mind in the slightest. He got quite friendly with me after this. "You're good for his lordship, sir," he said. "He'd lost his spark you know. Not like the old days." He licked his lips at the thought of it.
"What do you mean?" I said.
"I could tell you a tale or two sir," he said. But he didn't.

Later I tried to get his lordship talking about the past but he was pretty cagey. "You mustn't mind if Vladimir was rather fierce," he said. "It's in the family. I used to be rather fierce myself. Very fierce sometimes," and he smiled and patted me on the shoulder.

I tried to imagine him and his retainers and family driving away from the burning castle with the cartloads of gold. Josh told me Vladimir was only a baby. The attackers tried to block their way and they had to cut themselves out. David told Josh his lordship had hacked off six heads with his sabre. He said he picked up the last head and drank from it before he threw it at the remaining attackers who then ran for it. I found it difficult to believe this courteous old man could be the same person. He saw me looking at him and I think guessed my thoughts. He patted my arm again and said, "Different times require different things, and time and people change dear boy."

"Poor Vladimir didn't have a mother to bring him up," he added. "I think perhaps I didn't give him the attention he needed." Josh had told me that Big Drac's mother had been killed the night they were driven out. His lordship sighed. "I should have taken the time. I had plenty of it."

Well, there you are, bring your troubles to Eg. No one unreasonably refused. Three-hundred-year- old vampires a speciality. I said, "I wouldn't worry about your son. He seems able to take care of himself." And anyone else who gets in the way, I thought.

We had some good times, the old man and I, and we made a lot of noise. Big Drac and his wife didn't like it but said nothing. Dad thought it was funny. His bedroom was on the other side of the house. Josh and David wanted to join in but his lordship froze them out. He was very friendly but it was clear they weren't welcome. His lordship didn't have a lot of time for those two, and by the time we left he had even less.

CHAPTER 18

You don't have to try too hard to guess how Josh and little Drac disgraced themselves. Not content with bottles if not buckets of blood, they had to have a forbidden drink. I suppose that was the attraction. Josh said it was little Drac who led him on. The Dracs thought otherwise. So did I.

Boris brought them home. A very angry Boris. As he dragged them into his lordship's room I turned the music off. "I caught them red-handed my lord," he said. Red-toothed more like.

His lordship was really wild. He was cool with it though, just very calm and cold and white. He didn't say anything to them but spoke to Boris. "They must be punished," he said. "It's a serious matter. You know what to do. Put them downstairs."

So I came to visit the cellars of the house. Dungeons is the proper word really. It wasn't so bad down there. Not if you were just visiting. Not so good if you were chained to the wall though.

Josh and his friend didn't like it at all. Even Big Drac thought it was going over the top a bit. He came to talk to his lordship about it. I could see he didn't like me being there and he ignored me. "Look father," he said. "Don't you think it's a bit old fashioned chaining the boys up. We're not exactly in the old days are we."

His lordship sniffed. "A stitch in time saves nine, Vladimir. Better a night or two in irons than a stake through the heart. Or perhaps you don't remember the old days as clearly as you think." He paused and added, "You wouldn't hesitate if it was just the other boy". He was right there, Big Drac would have cheerfully chained Josh up and thrown the key away.

Mum was really annoyed. She didn't say much. She just pursed her lips and stopped talking to the Dracs. Dad thought it was quite funny. He said it would do Josh good. I didn't think it would do Josh any good at all but I thought it was a good idea and he deserved it.

Dad would have found anything quite funny. He was in a really good mood. He had had lots of visits to the capital city some way away, with and without Big Drac. "It's all set up," he said. "We're going to make money out of this and you and I," he squeezed Mum's arm, "won't have to be pin cushions any more." Free drinks for Josh. Hurray.

I enjoyed his lordship's company. Well, there wasn't anyone else worth talking to. We chatted a lot and I told him about our life at home and Saffron. And Tabitha. And on the last night I told him about Bag and how Josh had bitten him.

The old vampire sighed and for a moment looked even older, and for a while he was silent in thought. "It may mean nothing," he said. "I will pray for you." I wondered who or what he prayed to.

93

We left as we arrived, on a night flight. His lordship drove to the airport. "We're honoured father" said Vladimir. I think he meant it.

Before we left his lordship took me aside. "I want you to have this," he said. "This" was a thick but worn ring of gold set with a carved stone. "It is a family ring," he said. "It will be known to anyone in the family. It carries a little of my authority. Hide it in a safe place and only wear it if you need to." The old man was speaking in riddles but it was really nice of him to give me a present, although money would have been better than a ring I wasn't supposed to wear. I couldn't think when I'd need to wear a ring. Marriage seemed a long way off.
I said, "Thank you very much. I'll write and I'll send you some CDs."
His last words to me were, "Look after that brother of yours."

CHAPTER 19

Back home, home to a new life, my resolution was that I would not, under any circumstances, look after brother Josh. Well, it lasted longer than most of my resolutions.

It was Saffron I spent my time with. First to make sure she hadn't been got at by anyone else. Then to relax with her. I don't know why she liked me but she did and it was good. Let's not pretend. It was wonderful.

The weather was hot and we lazed in her garden and talked and snogged and went out in the evenings. And we swam, down at the open air pool in town. It was more like a club in the hot weather. Everyone was there. Everyone except Bag. Saffron said, "Thank God Bag isn't here showing off as usual." I didn't think. I just agreed and looked at her. Ignorance is bliss.

I couldn't get away from Josh, what with him going out with Saffron's sister. He was out of sight but not out of mind. Saffron said, "Can't you sort out that prat of a brother of yours. Tabitha is fed up with him. He won't go to the pool. He won't go out anyway, except in the evening. Your Josh may think he can get any girl but Tabitha will be off if he's not careful." She looked at me and said, "I don't know what it is about you and your wretched brother that gets Tabitha and me." She continued, "Just you hope it doesn't wear off, or we'll both be off with Bag." Thank you Josh I thought.

The next thing was the school Summer Fair. This took place a week before term started and was to raise money for the school. But it was good, and everyone went. There was a disco in the evening and we all went to that, Saffron and me and Josh and Tabitha.

I didn't recognise Bag at first. The disco strobes were whirling and flashing but even under those he looked awful. He was slouched in a chair. You can't keep a Scurf down though. He perked up when he saw Tabitha. He must have been feeling cunning rather than bullying tonight. He waited until Josh went off to the loo, and then in he was, asking Tabitha to dance. Well, what did Tabitha do? Laugh at him? Tell him to push off? Turn her back? Yes. She got up and danced.

Not that that did Bag much good. He wasn't moving well. His arms and feet were whirling away but it looked as if it was an effort. Then instead of slowing down he seemed to speed up until suddenly he stopped. Just like that. He stood stock still in front of Tabitha, his arms up, and then fell flat on his back.

That made everyone's evening. I can't think of anything else, apart from a proper bar, which would have made things go with such a swing. Josh was annoyed he'd missed it. It didn't seem to occur to him to ask what Tabitha was doing dancing with Bag.

96

Bag was well bevied. That was what everyone said. So did I. Well, it was a good few weeks since Josh had bitten him so it couldn't be that.

We had a near miss in the car park afterwards. Someone nearly reversed over Josh. Some poor father didn't see him in his mirror. I heard his wife giving him a right telling off: she'd drive next time, he shouldn't have had that extra glass and so on. I didn't interfere.

I think Bag liked people talking about him, which was just as well because there was a lot of it the next week. No sooner had people stopped talking about the dance than news came that he'd been taken off to hospital.
"In the middle of the night" said Tabitha.
"He's on a life support machine," said Saffron. We were sitting round the pool picking up gossip. Faced with the thought of no longer having to put up with Bag I felt just a little bit sorry for him.

It didn't last, I hasten to add. Any pity for Bag was quickly smothered by a growing feeling of worry nagging away at the back of my mind. I looked at Josh. His lips were pursed. Tabitha had dragged him protesting to the pool. He really liked her didn't he. Anyway, I couldn't see the expression on his face properly, what with a wide straw hat and the shades. But I knew what he was thinking. He wasn't worrying about Bag dying but about him staying dead.

Josh jumped up. "It's too hot for me. I'm going," he declared. And he went. Tabitha was gobsmacked. Her jaw hung open. Then it closed quickly and firmly and the muscles in her cheeks clenched. "That's it. That's it" she said. And she was off. Off round the pool chatting and smiling so a good few guys didn't know what had hit them. Well, there you are. As the fat lady at the vampire party said, mixed relationships don't work.˙ Poor old Josh, he wouldn't find another bird like Tabitha in a hurry. Not that I fancied her of course.

You will not be surprised that Bag's fate preyed on my mind. After a day it drove me towards Bag's house. This was on the edge of our little town, in a cul-de-sac backing on to fields. The sheep in the fields and the Scurfs got on well. They had a lot in common, though not as much as if the sheep had been pigs. The Scurfs' relations with their other neighbours weren't so harmonious. I'm not sure harmonious is the right word under the circumstances. Actually the Scurfs' band was really good, it's just that there's a time and place for everything.

The Scurfs' house was at the end of the cul-de-sac. It was a ramshackle place surrounded by sprawling outbuildings with corrugated iron roofs. The garden was full of rusty old cars. So was the roadside. The nearest neighbours were on the corner. I don't suppose they stood much chance of moving. Just imagine if you bought a house like that and got up on the first morning to find you had the Scurfs next door.

While I was congratulating myself on living somewhere else the Scurf door opened and out stepped Ma, shopping basket in hand. I quickly turned and retraced my steps. When I came to the local corner shop I stopped and looked in the window. Ma walked by and went into the shop. Nothing ventured nothing gained I thought, and followed her in.

"A bloomin' miracle that's wot" she said. "Dead they said 'e was. My boy. Dead. I can't tell yer 'ow I felt. And then fifteen minutes later they comes in and says Mrs. Scurf there's bin a mistake an' yore little boy's alright. Now, I'll 'ave two pounds of grapes and three boxes of them turkish delights wot 'e likes particular." And she slapped a £50 note on the counter.

My heart sank as I made my way home. When I got back Josh was moping about Tabitha. I tried to cheer him up. "She was always eyeing up other blokes behind your back," I said. But that didn't seem to cheer him up at all. I suppose it took his mind off Bag anyway. Lucky old Josh.

If this sounds a bit self pitying it is because I was feeling rather sorry for myself. It was back to carrying round the great secret on my own. Even Josh and I didn't speak about it. I think we felt if it was put into words it might be more likely to happen.

We went back to school and everything went smoothly. After a couple of weeks Bag came back to school. He looked pale and didn't have his usual bounce and confidence. The next day I knew we were in it. Someone had broken into the school overnight and broken all the mirrors in the boys' changing rooms.

That night I said to Josh, "We've got to talk about this. Bag's got it hasn't he? We'll have to talk to him". So we did.

We caught Bag at lunch time under the trees, off for a quick fag. We weren't welcome which wasn't surprising. "What d'yer jerks want" he said. But he had an uncertain look in his eyes.
"Having trouble with mirrors?" I said.
"Mind yer own business," he said. "I dunno who did it."
"If you'd looked in the mirror I don't suppose you'd have seen him," I said. That took his breath away. "Nice in the shade, isn't it," I added. "No nasty bright sun."
For a moment I thought he was going to cry. He bit his lip. "Wot d'yer know about it?" he said.
"A lot" I replied. "We'll meet you this evening. By the gravel pits." They were on the edge of town. I didn't want Bag near our house. Bag was a horrid secret and had better stay that way.

We met him at the gravel pits and walked through the woods surrounding them until we found a deserted clearing. He followed us like a lamb. Then we stood and faced one another. "Well" he said.

Josh and I had decided shock tactics were the only thing. I took a small bottle of blood from my pocket, uncorked it, and handed it to Bag. He frowned but as his brow went down his nostrils went up and his breath drew in with a hiss. He thrust the bottle into his mouth. Glug, glug. Down the hatch. Welcome to the night of the long tooths.

Bag stood there, open mouthed, teeth hanging out like baby elephants tusks, blood on his lips and a look of complete bewilderment on his face. His hand went up to his mouth and he felt it and his bright new teeth slowly and carefully as if he was in a dream.

But he looked better. He certainly did. The sag in his shoulders had gone and there was a hint of our old friend, if that's the right way to put it.

"You've become a vampire" Josh said. "So am I. I bit you in the fight, that's why you passed out. That's how you got it."

It wasn't easy. First he laughed. But he'd drunk the blood and felt the teeth and he knew about the mirror. Then he got angry. That was nasty. It was a good thing there were two of us. Then he panicked and got upset. That was easier to handle and we tried to explain everything to him. I don't think we got it across. As we parted Bag looked at me. "Yer 'aven't got it 'ave yer," he said. "Suppose I bite yer ter make it even."

CHAPTER 20

So Josh, Bag and I were drawn reluctantly into a sort of secret society and I got back to worrying big time. I wasn't worried about what happened to Bag. I'm nice but not that nice. You'd have to be very nice indeed to be concerned about Bag, unless you were another Scurf.

No, I was worried about what would happen if Bag was found out, or if he went round chomping on anyone who took his fancy. It seemed more than likely. And then what would we have? The police I suppose, the vivisectionists I daresay, and Big Drac and his friends.

How to keep Bag good and quiet, that was the question; and what were the answers? Blood, for a start. That meant we had to reduce Josh's ration to provide some for Bag. Fear was the other weapon. "Vampires see passing it on as a crime now" I said. "If you do that you'll be a threat to them and they'll do you in. That would be a pity when you could live for so long." Bag liked the idea of living for a long time.

We had to make Bag feel cheerful about what had been done to him. "Think of all the years you'll be able to collect your old-age pension" I said. That didn't impress him but he got the idea.
"I'll be pulling birds when you're an old man poking the fire," he said.

This prospect did not solve the immediate problem which was how to stop Bag chewing his way around town. So when Josh got his rations we had to pour some of the blood into a small plastic bottle. Josh couldn't be trusted with that so it was down to Eg to be the carrier of the blood, the keeper of the bottle. Eg also had to calm Josh down, a Josh made increasingly irritable by having his rations cut and seeing them passed to the enemy.

Usually we fed Bag at school. But one weekend he phoned us. Dad took the call. "Eg" he shouted. "Some yob on the phone for you."
Bag said, "I feel bad. I need some stuff. Yer've gotter bring me some."
"It's really not a good time," I replied.
"If yer don't I'll go and get some myself."
There was only one answer to that. "I'll be about an hour," I said.

And that's how I met the rest of the Scurfs. Ma opened the door. She was in a sort of nightie with a long greasy stain down the front. That might have come from the half-eaten chicken leg in her hand. She wiped her nose with the back of the other hand. "Ere, wotcha want?" she said.

"I've come to see Bag," I said. That set her back. I think the only people who'd ever called for Bag were policemen or social workers. She stood there for a bit, swinging the chicken leg absent-mindedly, taking in the idea that Bag had a friend and the Scurf family a genuine visitor.

Then a huge smile split her face. It quite changed her. "Bag" she shouted so the ornaments in the hall rattled. "Ere" she said, "come on in". And she led me down the carpet-tiled hall to the kitchen.

There were dirty dishes piled in the sink and dirty clothes in the corner of the floor by the washing machine. At the table sat Charlie writing away, his bass propped up against the table. I didn't think Charlie could read let alone write. Then I realised he was writing music.

Mum saw me looking. "Our Charlie's writin' our new number," she said proudly. "Pa's out late tonight but we're gonna practice it when 'e gets back." To Charlie she said, "'E's a friend of Bag's come ter visit." Charlie looked up surprised, nodded at me and went back to composing.

Bag came in. "Sorry ter keep yer Ma" he said. What the teachers would have given to have Bag like this. "Ello Eg," he said "nice ter see yer. Let's go up my room."

Bag's room was surprisingly clean and rather bare. There were posters on the wall and a second- hand stack system on an old chest.

And there were pictures, all Bag pictures I suppose, and some of them not bad at all. One showed a little Bag like figure disappearing down a sort of Doctor Who black hole. Perhaps that's how Bag felt about life. It certainly didn't look that way to the boys he terrorised at school.

Bag held his hand out for the bottle. Afterwards he said, "It ain't easy yer know. I'm used to bein' on me own but not like this, not at 'ome. I get so 'ungry, ... thirsty." He was silent for a bit and then said, "I know I can't go out bitin' strangers." Well, Bag kept to his word. He didn't bite any strangers. Just his family.

I got to meet all the Scurfs. It became embarrassing to talk to Bag at school. People started to comment about him. He took to wearing shades and started looking a bit like Josh. It just wasn't on for me to have a lot to do with him. But I had to get him the stuff. Three times a week I did it. Once at school and twice at his home.

It was hard work. Not the actual doing of it but how I felt about it inside my head. It took up all my thoughts and too much of my time. That's when Saffron went off, off with some bloke in a sports car. She was there like a fixture one minute and then she wasn't. She was very straight with me as always.
"You and your brother are a couple of weirdos," she said. "I've had enough of it."

I was pretty upset. Tabitha was good to me and chatted a lot. Actually I wasn't pretty upset, I was very upset. I remember one day I had to go to the dentist and have a filling. It's the only time I've enjoyed going to the dentist; the thought of it took my mind off Saffron. It might have been some consolation if this had overcome my worries about Bag but it didn't.

It was a lonely time. Lonely for me, for Josh and for Bag. I didn't realise how lonely for Bag it was until I saw the mark on his sister Sandra's neck. I'd gone round one evening to give Bag his you-know-what. Sandra came downstairs all done up and ready to go out for the evening. She looked what my Dad would have called all tarted up, and she had a little scarf round her neck.

We were in the kitchen with Freddie and Ma. "Ere" said Freddie. The Scurfs started most sentences off like that. "Wot yer got under there. Love bites?" and he pulled the scarf down. It wasn't a love bite but he wasn't far out.
"I dunno what it is," Sandra said. "It itches a bit."
"D' yer fink we've got fleas Ma?"
Great big ones with long teeth I thought.

I tried to reason with Bag. It was difficult because he didn't argue and agreed with whatever I said. I promised to increase his ration. I explained what could happen to Sandra. I might as well have talked to myself. Looking back I don't think it was the blood he was after. Bag was lonely. He wanted company.

It was at school several weeks later that someone came up to me and said Sandra had been taken off to hospital. "Just like Bag" they said. Surprise surprise. Later I heard that Sandra also had appeared to die and had come back to life, just like Bag. "They think it's some kind of virus," I was told. They weren't so far out.

106

It wasn't easy to keep up with Sandra and Bag together. Josh refused to talk about it. He buried his head in the sand. He also refused to reduce his rations any further. I was at my wit's end. I tried to persuade Bag and Sandra to split what we gave them but they said it wasn't enough. I realised there was only one thing for it.

So while Mum and Dad were out I swiped the syringe and one of Mum's nursing books. Josh was one thing. I'd never thought I'd be giving my life's blood to the Scurfs.

Sandra didn't seem to mind becoming a vampire. I suppose it was all in the family. I wondered if a few older men were going to get a nasty surprise on Saturday night. One more thing to worry about.

I needn't have worried. Sandra was very discrete about it. I was surprised. I didn't think she had the willpower. She didn't take a bite out of a single boyfriend. But it took her and Bag about six weeks to drink Ma dry.

Ma didn't go to hospital. When she collapsed Sandra and Bag tucked her up in bed and sat beside her, waiting with a cup of blood at the ready. When Ma woke up she took the blood, took it all in and took charge.

When I next knocked on the Scurf's front door it was Ma who opened it. "Right young Eg" she said. "Cummin 'ere an' tell me wot you've bin up to," and she led me into the kitchen where Bag and Sandra sat.

"Well," said Ma. "So we've got you ter thank fer all this then, eh?"
"Well it's Josh really" I said.
"Yes" she said. "O' course you ain't one of them, of us," and I'd swear she licked her lips as she looked at me. She pointed me to a chair so I sat down. She leaned over me with a leer. "Where is it?" she said, covering me with a blanket of b.o.
"What?" I said
"It," she said. "The stuff. You know, red and wet, and it ain't a newly painted pillar box."

I gave Ma the bottle. After all, what did it matter? It was helping me to get over my fear of needles I told myself. Help others and help yourself. She poured it into three glasses and they sat round the table slurping it and slapping their lips. Sandra and Ma hadn't got used to controlling their teeth yet and they kept sliding out. I watched this display of cannibalism with a sinking heart and hollow stomach. Hollow veins more like.

I will say, Ma seemed to have everything under control. "Our Sandra," she waved the glass at her, "you'd better get a night job. Somefink at the 'ospital. It's good money workin' nights and you'll be 'appier. Might even pick up a bit of free stuff." She raised her glass again. Then she turned to me.
"Now young Eg, where d'yer get this."
"It's Josh's rations," I said.

108

"Come on," she replied. "That brother of yours ain't given up all wot you've brought since our Sandra got took. Come on. Where's it from."

"Me," I said.

Ma lifted her glass and looked at it and sipped the dregs tasting them carefully. "Very nice stuff," she said. "Very kind of you I'm sure. Still you ain't gonna keep us all going on yer own are yer?"

There was no answer to that. Actually, there was, and Ma was on the ball.

"Our Bag 'ere says your Pa does deals in blood," she said.

Good old Josh I thought. Big-toothed and big-mouthed.

Ma was nice enough but very firm. She didn't expect the impossible but it must be possible to get blood and if we didn't, they'd get it where they could. Maybe she was bluffing. I didn't want to find out.

The first step was to drag Josh's ostrich head out of the sand. That wasn't too difficult. I just told him I'd have to tell Big Drac. Then we planned how to burgle Dad's office.

We were bound to be found out in the end I suppose, but we didn't worry about that. Only the present seemed to matter. We took a bottle at a time and made it last as long as possible. We had to take it to the Scurfs in smaller quantities, for anything we gave them they scoffed at once.

Josh and I took turns to go to the Scurfs, Josh having promised faithfully not to drink the stuff. He was getting more involved. He hadn't Tabitha to distract him and he kept well away from little Drac.

Bag had "joined the family", as they say. Sometimes I wondered whether we hadn't joined the Scurf family. One evening I knocked on the Scurf's door to have it opened by Sandra. She looked pretty good actually.
"'Ullo Josh," she said very cheerfully. When she saw it was old Eg her face fell.

I was on a downward path. A spot had appeared on my face. As I lay in bed trying to sleep I looked at my life. No Saffron, spots, and slavery to the Scurfs. I thought of becoming a vampire. At least I wouldn't be able to see myself in the mirror.

Ma took a bit of a fancy to me. I have all the luck! She'd sit me in the kitchen and chat. Sometimes she made my blood run cold. "Them boys," she said. "Good fer nuffink. Waste of eight pints of best." But she didn't mean it. At least I didn't think she did until Freddie got taken bad one day.

When I next visited Ma said, "Young Eg, we'll be needing more from now on won't we. I mean there's poor Freddie ter fink about." I thought about poor Freddie all night, and the sorcerer's apprentice and King Canute. The story of Eg's life; Dracula meets King Canute.

Josh wasn't much better. I think he must have dreamed about Frankenstein. He'd created a monster all right. Sometimes he'd panic.

110

"What are we going to do Eg?" he'd say.
"It can't get much worse," I said. But we both knew it could and would.

Some weeks later when I visited the Scurfs, they were sitting round the table. All except Pa. I handed over a whole bottle and they passed it round. That was when I noticed Charlie at the end of the table trying to control his new mouthwear. Ma said, "It's good bein' a family all together again i'nit." She paused and continued, "Mind, our Pa's lonely i'n 'e kids, eh?" Pa's days were numbered and so, it seemed to me, were Josh's and mine. We had come, as they say, to the end of the road.

CHAPTER 21

It was time to call for help. But while Josh and I planned how to tell Dad, Dad saved us the trouble. I was in my bedroom when he came home. "Josh!" he shouted. The shout was very loud and sounded unfriendly. I knew what had happened and I followed Josh downstairs.

Dad was beside himself. There was nothing to do but let him work through it. "Greedy rat ... ungrateful slob ... our lives upside down .... your mother ..." and on and on it went. Eventually he said to Josh, "Well, what have you got to say for yourself?"

Josh was silent but I said, "It wasn't for Josh, it was for the Scurfs."

Dad's eyes bulged and he tugged his hair frantically. Then he went white and sat down. "God almighty, what have you done," he said. So I told him.

"Why the Scurfs?" Dad kept repeating. "Why the Scurfs? Why not a bunch of lunatics, or some criminals, or some wild animals?". I tried to explain that the Scurfs weren't as bad as they seemed. But he didn't want to listen. "How are we going to tell your mother?" he said.

So we sat round the kitchen table. It wasn't a complete family meeting because Mum was away on a teaching course for a week. Whichever way we looked at it there seemed only one answer. "I'll have to divert a supply of blood," said Dad. "I don't blame you Josh, old chap. It was an accident. But it's a disaster." That wasn't exactly news to Josh and me.

Then Dad said what I'd been dreading. "I'll have to tell Vladimir." We did our best to persuade him not to. I thought of what the bearded man had said to big Drac at the party but I didn't repeat it. Dad said, "If Vladimir decides to have a go at the Scurfs it's his problem. It's Josh we have to protect." And that's exactly what I was worried about.

Dad, like all of us, was feeling a bit insecure and I think that's why he asked me to go with him to Big Drac's. Just in the car, of course, to chew it over there and back. I didn't stay in the car. I was there at the open window, not seen and not heard, but all ears.

Big Drac wasn't pleased, not pleased at all. Dad was really pally with him and thought he was being pally back but I could see it wasn't like that. I really got worried when big Drac did start to be nice to him, not really nice but pretend nice. Dad was so relieved he didn't realise.

Big Drac saw Dad to the door and then returned to the room. He went to the phone and dialled a number. "We have a problem," he said. "We must have a meeting. Tomorrow at 7p.m. I'll phone the others and arrange for them to come as well."

He put down the phone and I took off. The drive was empty but I found Dad parked at the gate.

"You were listening rat face," he said. "What did you hear?".

"Nothing," I said.

The next day was Saturday. Not a good day for Eg. I spent it worrying. I had a driving lesson in the afternoon. I was thinking about the great problem when I nearly ran an old lady over on a pedestrian crossing. "You won't pass your test like that," said my despairing instructor. "More like a free ticket to the crematorium. What's got into you?". He was right, that was the free ticket I was worrying about.

For the evening I invented a party that would keep me out late. Some party. I was strictly a spectator. I had to deliver the Scurfs' supply first so I left home early. Ma opened the door. "'Ello Eg" she said. "Pa's 'ad ter go ter bed. Not feelin' too good." And she gave a horrible laugh. I refused the offer of a cup of tea. I could just see them upstairs telling Pa how he could expect to live for centuries now. Little did he know. I went on to my next appointment.

When I got there, hidden outside the window, I could see Big Drac, the bearded man, and two other men I'd seen at the drinks do. They didn't look too happy. Big Drac paced the room. "There's no alternative Igor," he said to the bearded man.

"Are you sure?" said Igor. "I'm getting too old for this sort of thing."

"And I'm too old to move on again," snapped big Drac.

"You're his lordship's son," said Igor. "The decision has to be yours but I don't like it. Who's going to do the dirty work?"

Big Drac was chewing his fingers by now. Igor got up and put his arm round him. I noticed he had a limp.
"That was unfair," he said. "We depend on you in many ways. You must be kept out of it." Then he stood in thought and said, "We'll need six of us. We'll take the Scurfs in the night, coming from the fields. We'll do the business and then an explosion and fire I think. Is the gear in the cellar?"
Big Drac nodded, put his hand in his pocket and handed over a key.
Igor threw it to one of the others. "Fred, get the equipment."

There was a long silence while they waited for Fred to return. They might have been going camping but I knew they weren't. The sharp poles Fred carried weren't tent poles and I knew what the mallets were for.

I thought my blood was running cold but it froze solid when Igor said, "What about the other one, your David's friend. Have you organised that?"
"Yes," said Big Drac. "He's upstairs. David got him to come over here secretly. I didn't tell David why."
Igor shook his head. "Well, explaining it to David will be your problem I suppose. I'm glad it's not mine." Then he said, "What about the father?"

"We'll tell him a story," Big Drac said. "Anyway what can he do? We'll frighten him. We'll say if he doesn't keep quiet someone will bite the older son."
Charming, I thought. Dad certainly knew how to choose his business partners.

"If it had been the other one we wouldn't have had this trouble," said Igor. "I gather his lordship took a real fancy to him." Big Drac snorted. I could see he and I felt the same about one another. Igor continued, "We'll pay our visit at 2 a.m. when they're off their guard. We'll have to take the boy, what's his name? Josh, with us. We'll collect him later. You attend to your David. Lock him up. And you'd better stay here where we can contact you."

It was odd. Big Drac seemed to be the boss because of his father, but Igor seemed more in control and more impressive. "Very well Igor," said Big Drac.

They all left the room, and I left the window and fled.

CHAPTER 22

When I got back the house was in darkness. I found a note in the kitchen from Josh. It said, "Eg, Dad has had to go away unexpectedly on business. He'll be back tomorrow. I've been invited out to a party and I may stop over. Josh." Some party. A stake dinner.

What was I to do?

I spent some time first cursing myself for not telling Dad sooner.

Then I tried to work out where he could be, but the only business contact whose address I knew was Big Drac. Then I searched Dad's study for clues. No clues.

Then I looked for the bit of paper with details of Mum's course on it and the phone number, but Dad must have taken it with him.

Then I thought of another teacher who would know the address for Mum and picked up the phone.

Then I realised Mum couldn't do anything and put the phone down.

Then I thought of ringing the police. Excuse me, my brother has been kidnapped by vampires. Thank you sonny, run along now.

Then I went to my room and got the piece of paper from the bottom of my drawer and took it to the phone. And I rang his lordship.

They took ten minutes to answer. It was Boris. I could hear music in the background. "I'll get his lordship sir," he said.

It didn't take long to explain everything to him. Then he made me tell him about the meeting again. He wanted to know exactly what Big Drac and Igor had said. Then he made me describe where the Scurfs lived. "Two o'clock," he said. "And what is your local time now?"
I looked at my watch. "Half past eight".
"We haven't got long," he said.

"Can't you just ring your son and forbid it?" I begged. He sighed. "It's not as simple as that. I don't think a telephone call would do it. I know Vladimir. It would take something more than that."

There was a silence. Then he said, "I'll do what I can. I know people who will help. I'll be in touch." He added, "Remember the ring. It may help you."

It was the longest evening of my life. I felt helpless. Waves of panic came over me. And the clock ticked forward.

At eleven o'clock his lordship hadn't rung back. So I rang him again. I held on for twenty minutes but there was no reply.

I paced the house. Twice I picked up the phone to call the police and then put it down. At 1.15 I went to my room, found a thick jersey, and put on his lordship's ring.

At 1.20 I set off for the Scurfs.

CHAPTER 23

I think Igor and his men expected to overpower the Scurfs in their beds. Or perhaps chatting over a late-night cup of cocoa. But then he didn't know much about the Scurfs. As I reached the corner of their road I wondered if Igor and his friends were already hidden in the dark fields beyond and what they made of chez Scurf.

Every light in the house was on and from it came the sound of the Scurfs in full practise, belting it out. I thought of Josh out there somewhere in the fields, braced myself, and walked up the path.

It took five minutes to make them hear and then only because they were in between numbers. Ma opened the door. "'Ello young Eg, couldn't yer sleep? Got anyfink for us?" And she winked at me. Then she said, "'Ere, yer look dreadful. Wots the matter?" Not as dreadful as you may look in half an hour I thought.
"It's an emergency," I said. "I've got to talk to all of you".

Ma led me to the kitchen. Here the table had been pushed to one side for the jam session. They were high. High on music and high on blood. I'd recognise the look anywhere. Where had they got it? I looked round. Pa wasn't there. He was resting upstairs, with half-empty veins, waiting to join the family.

As I walked into the kitchen there had been a blast of sound as the next Scurf number started. But the music trailed away as one by one they saw something awful in my face. I said, "The vampires have found out about you. They've got Josh and they're coming to get you."

"Huh," said Ma. "It'll take more than a few old grave robbers to see off my boys. Ain't that right my dears?"

But nobody answered the question. Instead the back door opened. In walked Igor followed by three others. They all carried nasty looking clubs. The Scurfs stood frozen like waxworks.

Igor said, "A full house. Go and let Kurt in at the front door. And find the father." One of the men left the kitchen. Igor looked at me and nodded wearily. "We saw you come in. How did you find out?"

"I listened at the window," I said.

He shook his head, "You'd have been better off not being here."

Inside my head I went into another session of cursing myself. Why hadn't I told Dad, why hadn't I told the police, above all why hadn't I told the Scurfs in time? But that wouldn't have helped Josh. At least I knew where Josh was now. Outside with the sixth man. Sure enough the door opened and through it walked Josh with his keeper, gagged and with bound hands. While the Scurfs watched open-mouthed, Josh was gently pushed on to a chair.

121

It seemed liked a dream, a nightmare. Before we awoke from it they seized Charlie and Freddie and tied their hands behind their backs. Bag backed into a corner raising his fists. Nobody spoke. It happened like a silent film.

Then Sandra screamed. One of the men seized her and put his hand over her mouth. Ma went wild. "You leave our Sandra alone," she shouted and went for them. Bag piled in beside her. They overpowered him easily enough but it took all five of them to fix Ma. What a fight she put up. There was this struggling mass in the middle of the kitchen with Ma in the middle. She kept coming to the top and then going down. When she surfaced for the last time she fixed her teeth firmly in the nearest neck.

Ma wouldn't have lasted a minute against Igor but he stood at the door, unsmiling, watching and frowning.

At last Ma was trussed up and put on a chair. She moved her lips as if she had a nasty taste in her mouth and wrinkled her nose in disgust. "Yuck," she said, and looked at Kurt who was nursing his wound in his neck. "Wot yer got in them veins of yours, somefink wot the cat left behind?" she added.

And what was our hero doing? Did he join in the fight? Did he defend Sandra? Did he help Ma? Did he escape and go for help? No. Our hero quivered and cowered at the side of the kitchen. He wasn't even worth tying up.

Then I heard someone speak. It sounded a long way away. Then I realised it was me. The voice said, "You can't do this. I forbid it. His lordship would forbid it and I forbid it in his name."

Igor gave me a very tired look. "You can't forbid it and his lordship isn't here. It was a mistake for you to come."

I thrust my hand at him. "I've spoken to him" I said. "On the phone. He told me to do this. To forbid you to do what you planned."

Igor took my hand and looked at the ring for a long time. Then he said, "I haven't seen that for many years." He was deep in thought. I thought I was getting somewhere when he said, "Kurt, tie this young man up."

I looked at Igor and thought as quickly as I could. I said, "You were with him when he fought his way out, from the castle, when Big Drac, I mean Vladimir, was a child."

"You know a lot," he said.

Kurt had got hold of me.

"Let him go," said Igor.

I continued desperately. "You're not happy about this. Vladimir is a boy to you. You don't have to do what he says."

"That's it," said Ma. "You listen to 'im."

"He's still my liege lord," said Igor. "Old habits die hard."

"So is his lordship," I said. "Only more so. I spoke to him on the phone this evening. He forbids it. He said find another way."

"So you say," said Igor. He paced up and down. "Let's ring his lordship ourselves then".

So we did but there was no reply. Then Igor said, "Vladimir will have to come after all. You can try to persuade him." He turned, "What did you call him?"

"Big Drac" I said. "Short for Dracula".

Igor barked a laugh, "There's many a true word spoken in jest," he said.

Igor picked up the phone again. We heard his half of the conversation. "Vladimir, there's a problem .... the boy Egbert is here. He has your father's ring and claims its authority. He says your father forbids it .... well, you'll have to come .... no, it has to be your decision ..... no, Vladimir that's the ring on which I pledged myself to your father. You come over here and sort it out .... don't park in the front, walk across the fields ... all right, thirty minutes."

He put the phone down. "You've got half an hour to think of an alternative."

"You can trust us," said Ma. "Ain't that right boys?"

"Yea, that's right," they said.

Sandra undid a button of her dress and sort of wriggled her shoulders giving a flashing smile to Igor but he didn't seem to notice. I heard him mutter, "What a mess."

"Well," said Ma. "Wot about a nice cuppa tea? 'Ere why don't yer let me go and I'll do one fer all of us."

She looked very humble and un-Ma-like as she said, "I won't cause no trouble, honest."

"No shouting," said Igor.

"Blimey no, no shoutin'," said Ma.

"Still, I think we'd better have some noise," said Igor. "Put some music on.

"Ere, why don't yer put on the tape wot we done of Charlie's new numbers?" said Ma.

So Ma was cut free to make tea and the Scurf sounds rang out again down the road. Everything was back to normal apart from the burial squad taking its cup of tea.

Ma served them first. Then she served us. As she gave me my cup she winked at me. Igor left his tea untasted on the table.

There wasn't a lot to say. We sat or stood until big Drac arrived. He came through the back door in a filthy mood. Ma picked up Igor's luke warm cup and thrust it at him. "Ere, 'ave a cuppa tea," she said. I thought he was going to throw it at her and I think he was but thought better of it. He gulped it and pushed the cup back at her rudely, making a face.

"What's she doing untied?" he said, "and him?" he added, pointing to me.

I held the ring up at him. "You mustn't do it," I said. "I've got your father's ring. He told me to use it."

"What does he know?" said Big Drac. "He's past it."

He could see this didn't go down well with Igor, and changed his tune, putting his hand on the bearded man's shoulder. He said, "Igor my friend, I don't like

125

it any more than you but it has to be done. And my father has done worse in his time and so, I've heard, have you."

As I saw Igor's shoulders sag I knew I'd lost. There was only one thing for it. The sink was at my back and by its side the kitchen drawer. I turned, pulled it open and grabbed a kitchen knife.

I backed towards the door, knife arm stretched out. "Don't tell me," said Igor. "You're going to get the Police". He was dead right. I was going to do what I should have done in the first place.

Igor gave a little smile. By him stood a rusty umbrella stand. He took a walking stick from it and pointed it at me. He took a step forward crouching like a fencer. The stick sort of wound round the knife and it whipped from my fingers, up, up and fell to the floor. Igor looked apologetic. "Sorry about that," he said. "Two hundred years of practise. Don't feel bad about it."

I did feel bad about it, very bad. I bolted for the door, got it open and rushed through it. My speed was increased by Igor's weight behind me. I landed face down on the ground with him on top of me, my hopes in ruins and my face in the mud.

I lay there winded and in despair, a buzzing in my ears. The buzzing got louder, a familiar sound I couldn't put a name to. I heard Igor exclaim and heard and felt him get up.

Crawling to my feet I raised myself up to stand by Igor's side, both looking upwards. I would have been no more surprised by a flying saucer as I watched a huge helicopter descend into the Scurf's backyard.

CHAPTER 24

As the helicopter descended, the noise grew louder and those who were free to do so tumbled out of the back door to see what was going on. By that, I mean those who weren't tied up; that is to say Big Drac, Igor and his gang, Ma and Sandra.

The blades of the helicopter swung more slowly as the engine stopped. The door opened and two men dropped to the ground.

I looked at the first one. He wore jeans and a leather jacket, studded like a biker's, but elegant. He was wearing a pair of wicked trainers I could never afford and round his neck were his earphones. Was it a bird, was it a plane, was it the Seventh Cavalry? No folks, it was his lordship.

He said, "Hello, dear boy, just in time by the looks of things." He looked round, taking it all in. "You weren't difficult to find," he said. "The only house in town with all the lights on." I wondered what the Scurf neighbours were making of all this. Just another Saturday night I daresay.

By his lordship's side stood Boris. He was in one of his butler type outfits: black jacket, tie, white shirt and striped trousers. Both of them wore an article of dress I would not have expected. From the waist of each of them hung a long slightly curved sword.

Vladimir didn't like it. And I don't think he liked his lordship speaking to me first. "What the hell are you doing here father?" he said. The old man's eyes flashed. "I've come to see what you're up to Vladimir."

"I'm clearing up the mess your friend's brother has made," said Big Drac sharply, "and you're not going to stop me."

His lordship turned to Igor. There was a troubled look on Igor's face as his eyes went from his lordship to Big Drac and back again. His lordship spoke quietly to Boris who unsheathed his sabre and handed it to his master. Holding it by the blade his lordship offered the sword to Igor.

"Here my friend," he said. "You must decide which end to hold out and who is your lord." He smiled and added, "We never found out which of us was the best swordsman." Igor took the sword reversed it and handed it back to his lordship hilt first. Then he went down on one knee and kissed the ring on his lord's hand.

"That's better," said the old vampire and raised Igor. "Now what were you saying Vladimir?"

If Big Drac had been anyone else I would have felt sorry for him. Here he was being the big boss and his Dad turns up and treats him like a kid in front of everyone. But Big Drac wasn't anyone else and I really enjoyed it.

Ma had been taking everything in. She knew which side her bread was buttered. "Pleased ter meet yer yer worship. Would yer like a cuppa tea, dear?" I thought his lordship would put her in her place but he said, "That would be very kind of you." He added, "Shall we go in now?"

As we filed into the kitchen I could see his lordship's head nod to the music in approval but he was distracted only for a moment. He pointed at Josh. "Igor, put this young man who's caused all the trouble in the helicopter." As Josh passed by, his hands still tied behind his back, his lordship said to him, "Thank your brother, young man", and to Igor, "Tie him to the seat in there." To me he said, "I think your brother had better come to stay with me for a while. He'll be safer there, and he needs to learn some manners and ways he can't be taught at home." He patted me on the shoulder. I'll come and see your parents and sort it all out."

Five pairs of Scurf eyes were locked on his lordship's face, trying to see their fate. He looked at the anti-vampire equipment in the corner and pursed his lips. Then he said, "Is there somewhere we can talk".
Ma said, "There's the living room, yer worship. I'll bring yer tea in there shall I?"

So his lordship, Big Drac, Igor, Boris and I sat in the living room. Why me? Big Drac thought that too. "What's he doing here?" he said.
"If it weren't for my friend Egbert I wouldn't be here," said his lordship as if that made everything all right. Looking at Big Drac I could see that so far as he was

concerned it made things even worse. But he shut up.

Ma brought the tea in. His lordship sipped his cup. When she'd left the room he put it down and said, "I just got here in time."
"But how did you do it" I said.
Big Drac answered. His voice was bitter. "My father has his own aircraft and a pilot's licence but he doesn't visit here very often." He addressed his lordship, "I suppose you hired the helicopter and flew it directly on from the airport." His lordship nodded. I was impressed. It was a lot more practical than turning yourself into a bat. "He pleases himself," said Big Drac. He pleases me too, I thought.

"A fine mess you were going to make of this Vladimir," said his lordship. "We're not back in the castle you know. There's a police force here. What were you going to do, do the business and blow them up?"

There was a guilty silence. "Really?" he said. "I can just see the headlines. Ritual murder of whole family. How did you think you'd get away with that. You've got no imagination. As for you Igor, I can't think of anyone I'd prefer by my side in a battle but you'd best leave the planning to someone else and I don't mean Vladimir."

Igor looked humble. I felt more cheerful by the minute. His lordship was at least one vampire who'd left the Middle Ages behind. Then he said, "No, we've

131

got to get them out of here and finish them off somewhere else quietly."

I couldn't help myself. I said, "You mean kill them?" He looked at me curiously. "What else?" he said. "Don't worry, your brother will be quite safe but these peasants cannot be trusted. They have to go. Sad but necessary. We'll take them with us and pop them out of the plane over the sea. We'll have to leave one of them behind to tidy up and explain to the neighbours but we can deal with him or her later."

Hello Middle Ages I thought. This should please Big Drac. Grudgingly he said, "Well, I suppose that's all we can do now. Your helicopter isn't exactly going to go unnoticed." He spoke very slowly and then he yawned and shook his head.

There was a silence, and in the silence we heard movement in the other room. Boris was on his feet in a flash and through the door followed by Igor. His lordship followed more slowly. Big Drac stayed in his chair, his hand to his head. Odd, I thought as I passed him on my way to the kitchen.

In there I saw Boris blocking the back door. On the other side of the room sat Charlie and Freddie still bound to their chairs. In front of them stood Ma, Sandra and Bag. A cut end of rope was hanging from one of Bag's wrists. In Ma's hand was a familiar looking kitchen knife which she was waving vigorously.

And what about Igor's gang? They were fast asleep, in the land of nod, two in chairs and three on the floor.

Ma had evidently been able to hear through the door. "Peasants!" she said. "Who d'yer fink you are, callin' us peasants! Call yerself a lord and goin' round dressed up ridiculous like that. Peasants! Well mate you don't get rid of the Scurfs that easy."

Ma seemed more annoyed at being called a peasant than by the prospect of being pushed out of a plane. You had to admire her.

But Boris, Igor and his lordship were more than a match for Ma, Bag and Sandra. I wondered if I would make a difference to their chances but Boris took his sabre out and I could see it was hopeless. I could only think of one thing to do. I took off the ring and gave it to his lordship. I said, "What you're doing isn't right. You'd better have this back." He narrowed his eyes and looked thoughtful.

A voice came from behind us. "Can't you turn that dreadful row off?" I turned round. Big Drac was in the doorway; hanging on to the doorway would be more correct. He looked dreadful. He kept stifling a yawn. In between yawns he said, "Turn that awful noise off someone."

Ma hopped from one foot to the other and waved the knife in the air. "That ain't no noise," she shouted. "You ain't got no respect and no taste neither. That's

133

our latest tape wot we recorded and it's our Charlie's latest number wots on now."

Big Drac sort of groaned and lurched back into the living room. His lordship only had attention for Ma. "Excuse me, my good woman. What did you say?"
"I ain't your good woman you toffee nosed git," shouted Ma, "an' that's our tape, our music wot we recorded."
"Who is 'we'?" asked his lordship, not at all put off by Ma.
"We is us," shrieked Ma, waving at the others.
"That's right," said Sandra.

His lordship took a step forward towards Ma. Bag jumped in front of her. "Don't you touch our Ma you dirty old man!" he shouted. Freddie and Charlie were still gagged so they didn't say anything.

"My dear lady," said his lordship. "I wouldn't dream of hurting you. But is it really true, that your family made this wonderful sound?"
Ma looked suspicious. "Wots yore game, then?" she said.
His lordship looked round the kitchen, seeing the instruments. "Those are what you play?" he asked.
"We don't 'oover the floor with 'em," said Ma grimly.
His lordship stood back and waved an arm at Igor. "Untie them and give them their instruments. He drew up a chair and sat down. "Play," he commanded.

Igor cut Charlie and Freddie free. "Ere" said Ma. "We're not like somefink on the Titanic yer know. We ain't playin' fer yer while the ship goes down."

"Play," said his lordship. Boris drew his sabre half out of the scabbard. Suddenly the band was getting itself together briskly. Ma was sitting at the drums when she said, "We ain't got Pa, 'e's on the guitar. Oh my god, wot's happened to Pa." She got up. "I gotta see 'ow Pa is." Boris waved her down. "Play," he said.

So the Scurfs played. They played as if their lives depended on it, which as it turned out was quite correct.

The first number ended. Ma said, "Now we gotta vocal for Sandra." Sandra undid another button and took a deep breath but before a word came out there was a hammering on the front door. His lordship just said "Boris," and Boris went down the hall to the door. I followed him. He opened the door in mid - knock.

A tirade of abuse came through the door. "I'll have the law on you ... yobs .. gypsies..there's decent folk can't sleep..house unsaleable....police." The voice trailed away. Boris stood in his black jacket, striped trousers and sabre. "Can I help you sir?" he said.

I watched the neighbour stagger back down the path scratching his head and trying to convince himself he was in the middle of a bad dream. I wondered what he'd say to his wife when he got home. Did you tell them dear? Not exactly but I left a message with their new butler. I didn't like to be too rude because he was wearing a sword. Boris and I returned to the kitchen in time to catch the end of Sandra's number.

"Wonderful" his lordship said. "Wonderful. What instrument does your father play"?

Ma liked that and gave him a horrible leer. Disgusting. You'd think old people would be past that sort of thing. She said, "Pa plays the guitar." After a hesitation she added, "'E's me 'usband actual. 'E's a lot older than me." About three or four days I would have thought.

His lordship rose from his chair. "I wonder if I might join you. I used to play the classical guitar many years ago, and recently", he turned and smiled at me, "I have been practising a more modern technique."

Ma knew who was the boss. "We don't 'ave no techniks dear but yer can borrow Pa's electric guitar. Come up 'ere."

He wasn't bad, he wasn't bad at all. He played in with them like an experienced musician. And when a vocal number came up he took over the chorus with a gravelly voice.

"Marvellous" he said again at the end of the number and put the guitar down. Boris and Igor still guarded the doors leading from the kitchen and Igor held his lordship's sabre.

"Sit down, sit down," said his lordship genially, as if talking to honoured guests rather than those about to die. I could see the Scurfs wondering whether to make a run for it. But a kitchen knife wasn't much good against a sabre and they stayed put.

His lordship was in a very good mood now. "Well my friends," he said. "There is no problem, no problem at all. You can all come and stay with me."

"An' wot if we don't want ter," said Bag defiantly.

"Ah" said his lordship. "Do we really need to go into that?" Bag looked at the stakes in the corner of the kitchen and decided this was good advice.

"'Ere," said Ma. "I know wot yer up ter. I 'eard wot you said in there. Stay wiv you. Get chucked out of yore plane more like."

"No, no my dear lady" he replied. "You'll all be quite safe. This," he waved his hand at the instruments on the floor, "changes everything."

"Yer don't want no peasants in yore 'ouse," said Ma grimly.

"Such rudeness," said his lordship. "Please forgive me. No peasant could play like that. Anyway times change. Sometimes I forget when it is."

Ma looked at me. "'E's the big cheese then?"
"The boss," I replied. "He's very old."

137

Ma looked approving at this. She said, "Can we trust 'im?" I looked at his lordship. He handed the ring back to me without a word. "You can trust him," I said.

"Will you accept my hospitality?" said his lordship.

"Well," said Ma. "We can't stay 'ere no more, that's fer sure. There's a lot of us and we ain't got no stuff, no blood, an' we're bound ter get caught. And when yore gone there's still this lot after us." And she pointed to the sleeping vampires.

Having made the decision, Ma thought she'd better sound a bit more grateful and continued, "'Ain't 'is worship 'ere a perfick gent. An' e seems to 'ave plenty of dosh an' I expeck he 'as a lovely big 'ouse wiv lots of room fer us, ain't that so?"
"That's so," I said.

"Well then say fank you ter 'is worship," said Ma to the Scurfs, and they did.

Then his lordship said to Ma, "Dear lady, now that we are on the same side perhaps you could tell me what you have done to my friends." He waved at the sleeping beauties and over his shoulder to the living room from which big Drac's snores could be heard.

"Knock out drops" said Ma proudly. "Pa's sleeping mixture. 'E can't sleep yer know. 'E 'as ter 'ave extra strong stuff. I put it in the tea." She pointed at Igor.

"E wouldn't drink it but we could 'ave fixed him on 'is own." Some hopes.

Ma contemplated her lost victory, thought better of it and said, "We're much better off going off wiv you than bashin' this lot up. Is it 'ot where you live?"
His lordship nodded.
Ma continued, "I fought it must be because you look sort of tanned for one of them, one of us. Pa's goin' ter love this." Then Ma clapped her hand to her head. "Oh my gawd – Pa!" she exclaimed.

CHAPTER 25

I saw Igor give a warning glance to his lordship and the two of them followed Ma who rushed up the stairs now she was free to do so. Nosey as ever, I followed, and behind me, a line of Scurfs.

As we got to the room, I heard a howl from Ma. "'E's gone," she cried.

For a moment I thought Pa had escaped. When I got in the room I saw that he had, in a manner of speaking. Pa had made his last deal. There he was, in his bed, as dead as a doornail.

This was my first experience of death. If you think I took it lightly that is because a single natural death was a pleasant contrast to what I had been expecting earlier.

It was a sad business even if it was old ferret face. Ma and the other Scurfs were very fond of him so he must have had some good points.

Ma turned on Igor at one point and said, "'E might be alright if you 'adn't come."

But Igor said, "I'm afraid not. It happens sometimes, especially with older people, that their bodies cannot survive the change and they die. We know of no cure for it."

His lordship took Ma by the arm. "Igor is right," he said. "We are all very sorry". I found it weird. One minute they'd come to put a stake through his heart and the next they were saying they were sorry he was dead.

Soon people were talking about funeral arrangements. His lordship was saying that of course the Scurfs must stay for a week to sort their affairs out. And then Ma offered to put his lordship up and he accepted.

"You can say I'm a relation," said his lordship. Who was going to believe that I thought. Still if he didn't speak and kept his leather jacket on. "'Ere, we can't call yer yer worship if we're related," said Ma.

"You can be our gran'pa" said Sandra cheerfully "now we ain't got no Pa." So grandpa it was.

And where was brother Josh while all this was going on? Tied-up and forgotten and serve him right I daresay. Or at least forgotten until Boris was ordered to take the helicopter back. Yes, Boris had a pilot's licence too.

By the time Josh came in rubbing his wrists and hungry for explanations it was nearly dawn. As we stood in the Scurfs' backyard, watching the helicopter rise into the still air, the sun edged over the horizon.

"And now," said his lordship, "We must take our friends home." I could see that 'we' didn't include

141

him. I could also see that he was looking at Igor and me.

Ma said, "Yer wonta stick them geezers in the back of the van". And that's what we did, using the Scurfs battered Transit.

Before we left, his lordship said, "I suppose I'd better telephone Vladimir's wife and say he's on his way." He looked at me and added, "You know, dear boy, I've never really got on with her. I'm sure it's my fault." But he was sure it was her fault and I expect it was. So Josh, Igor and I half carried and half persuaded Big Drac and his gang into the van and Igor drove them home. I have to say I enjoyed dropping Big Drac off. Mrs Drac was in a right state. I said, "He's had a few too many." But I didn't say what of.

Igor drove us home. When the car stopped he said, "His lordship has changed. He's more like he was in the old days, more life in him, but gentler." He laughed, "A lot gentler." To Josh he said, "Count yourself lucky." To me he said, "I'll be seeing you." But it was a while before I saw Igor again.

CHAPTER 26

It was light when Josh and I unlocked our front door. We sat in the kitchen and I gave Josh a blow by blow account of what had happened. I didn't miss out any of the nasty bits. If Josh had to go it was best he went willingly.

Afterwards Josh crashed out. I was tired but not able to sleep. Dad got back mid-morning and I filled him in. I did miss the nasty bits out for him. Why worry him unnecessarily? "It's a great chance for Josh," I said, "really wicked". Dad pulled at his hair and looked as if he didn't know what to do. "I don't know what your mother will say," he said.

We found out what Mum would say when she returned from her course after lunch. "No, no and no. That old monster isn't taking our baby away. What would he do with Josh, keep him chained up in the cellar. And with the Scurfs, ugh!"

I could see this was going to be difficult. They had to be told more. So I explained that while Josh did have a choice it wasn't much of one. He'd always be in danger from Big Drac and his friends and they'd be bound to get him in the end. It was either life of luxury with his lordship or a free tent pole and a trip to the cemetery.

That put the cat among the pigeons. Mum started crying. Dad kept asking questions and in the end I told them everything. At some point the whisky bottle appeared on the table. I could see they were

143

going to grind on for hours. I was exhausted and left them to it. As I closed the kitchen door behind me Dad was pacing around waving his glass in the air and Mum was sitting at the kitchen table with her head in her hands.

I got up late afternoon. Mum and Dad were still at it although the whisky bottle had disappeared. Josh was there too. It was all very boring.

I went into the hall and rang the Scurfs' number. Boris answered. He must have returned from the airport. "This is the Scurf residence," he said. I asked for his lordship. When he came on I said, "There's a lot of trouble over here. Mum doesn't want to let go of Josh. I thought you might be able to explain it to them better."
"My young friend Egbert," he said. "It will be no trouble at all and a much shorter journey than your last telephone call required."

His lordship came round in his posh clothes. Dad fussed around him. "Would you like a drink, er, sherry, wine, whisky or we've got some er, some er, er, what we give Josh."
"That'll do nicely," said his lordship. "And I'll have a whisky in it if I may."
His lordship took out a huge cigar. "Do you mind if I smoke?" he asked.
"No" said Mum and Dad who do go crazy if anyone smokes in the house.

"I will care for him like my own son" he said. That badly I thought. "He has a talent for languages," he

144

continued. "Once he has mastered that he can go to the school and then university."

This was all music to any Mum and Dad's ears. Dad started making grateful noises but Mum was still mistrustful.

"Of course,"added his lordship, "there is the business you have set up with Vladimir. I'm sure I can help with that. And it is most important that the two brothers keep in touch. I would be pleased to pay for Egbert to come and stay in the holidays, and at half-term if you would let him. And, of course, yourselves. I hope you will accept my hospitality."

I could see Mum giving in. Dad said, "You're very kind." I said, "Why are you so kind?"

His lordship replied, "Josh's great grandfather was one of my followers and his great grandmother was, so to speak, introduced to our "family" by myself. And as for you, dear boy; well, you have opened a new window onto the world for me, and it is I who am indebted to you."

Dad told Josh's school that he had to go away for health reasons, which was true enough, and that he was to stay with relations. We kept the connection with the Scurfs quiet.

Which was just as well because the news of the Scurfs' departure was celebrated all over town. Celebrated was the word all right. I went to Pa's funeral. Afterwards we went back to the Scurfs' for

145

tea. It wasn't a big party. Just the Scurfs, his lordship, Boris and me. We agreed Josh should stay away.

As we drove past the Scurfs' neighbours I could see that another bigger party was in progress. One person had put flags out in front of his house. As we went by several people waved glasses at us. Ma was philosophical about it. "Well, we'll get a lot more for the 'ouse if we ain't in the neighbourhood," she said.

Ma had prepared the funeral tea. His lordship contributed a large bottle of you know what and introduced the Scurfs to the ultimate whisky cocktail. Things got very lively. There was a nasty moment when I told Freddie he wouldn't be able to collect his unemployment benefit abroad. Then Ma and Sandra started crying about Pa.

It took Bag to say, "'Ere Ma, why don't we play a few numbers fer Pa?" And so they did with an audience of his lordship, Boris and me, and the sound bursting out of the open windows to mingle with the music of the neighbours' party.

It was a week of farewells. Everyone fussed round my rat of a brother. New clothes, new shoes, new shades, new everything. He was unapologetic about it. "It makes them happy," he said. "Gets their guilt off."

Sometimes I get this warm glow that makes me feel good about doing something which I then bitterly regret. That's how I felt when I bought Josh a goodbye present.

Josh had a passport but the Scurfs hadn't. The biggest trip they'd ever been on had been to the seaside. "No problem," said his lordship. "See to it Boris," and it got seen to.

Josh wanted to take his synthesizer with him. Mum and Dad told him it would be far too expensive. But when his lordship came round Josh worked it into the conversation. "Synthesizer? You play?" said his lordship. "Why didn't you tell me?" he said to me.

Then what does his lordship say? "Oh, leave it here, we'll get you another one." I thought of asking Josh to bite me hard.

They went two days after the funeral. I left Mum and Dad slobbering over Josh as I set off for the Scurfs.

Ma opened the door. "'Ello Eg," she said as she gave me a big hug. I noticed that she didn't smell. Well, it's an ill wind as they say.

A bit later over a cup of Scurf tea, perhaps the last, she said, "We owe you Eg. You'll collect one day."

"That's right," said Sandra, and she sort of fondled the back of my neck so I felt very uneasy.

I could hear the helicopter faintly through the open window. Ma looked at the kitchen table, which was covered in dirty plates. "Ain't much point in washin' this lot up is there," she said.

We stood in the back yard as it landed. It was huge, which was just as well since a lot was to go into it.

Josh, Boris and his lordship got out. Boris said to me, "I hope we see you soon sir. Don't worry, I'll look after your brother, make sure he doesn't do what he shouldn't." I hoped he had his ball and chain well oiled. He was going to need it.

His lordship shook my hand. "You'll be hearing from me soon. And I'll book your flight over for the holiday. I got the date from your father."

Josh said, "Goodbye Eg, see you soon."
I said, "Look after yourself." I thought, good riddance. I didn't mean it really.

Bag looked me in the eye and said, "'Ere Eg, fanks a lot. You can 'ave my posters. Give my love to Tabitha. I fink she fancies yer yer know."

Sandra gave me a big sloppy kiss, which I quite liked.

Charlie almost broke my hand when he shook it.

Freddie said, "'E's not such a bad old geezer is 'e? Amazin' voice!" And then he flashed his teeth at me. Very bad manners I thought.

Ma enveloped me in another pneumatic hug. "You get on wiv yore studies young Eg, yore going ter make somefink of yourself, not like this lot."

I stood there waving till the dot in the sky vanished.

Then I went in and washed the dishes.

On the way home I dropped the house keys in at the estate agents.

I felt lonely.

But I needn't have worried. I wasn't going to get rid of brother Josh and the Scurfs that easily.

BOOK TWO

GIVE US A HAND

CHAPTER 1

Term had ended and I was on the plane, going to see Josh. You would have thought after all the trouble I'd had with Josh and the Scurfs that I'd have been pleased to see the back of them. But in a funny sort of way I missed them all.

If you mix with bad company you get used to it I suppose. Tabitha, Josh's ex-girlfriend was the same. Whenever I saw her she wanted to talk about them. Why, I don't know, since she dumped Josh before he went, and always said she didn't like Bag. But I enjoyed chatting about them with her. It took me a while to realise that what I was enjoying most was Tabitha's company. By then I'd really fallen for her and she seemed to like me too.

Boris collected me from the airport. "There have been a lot of changes," he said with a broad smile. There certainly had. The first one was Ma. She'd lost so much weight and really smartened herself up, and she didn't smell. "'Ullo young Eg," she said. "Come ter 'elp? There's plenty ter do." She was right.

The ballroom was being altered and building materials lay everywhere. It was early morning and the workmen had just started. Ma was ordering them round. They were a frightened lot and kept crossing themselves.
"I weren't never no good at school," she said. "But this language is real easy. Gran'pa learns me and I got plenty of practice with this lot", and she shouted

directions at a passing workman.

"What are the alterations for?" I said.

"That's the surprise," she said with satisfaction. "It's goin' ter be a nightclub, a bloomin' nightclub, an' we're all goin' ter play in it."

The warm climate seemed to suit the Scurfs. From being a load of layabouts they had become fitness freaks. Even Bag. He'd be up at the crack of evening; working out, lifting and leaping and then off for a five mile jog. I wouldn't fancy Josh's chance against him now, although Josh still kept himself fit. But there was no need to worry. He and Bag seemed to be great friends.

Bag was also drawing. Not graffiti. I think that would have earned him the chance of decorating the dungeon. No, Bag was drawing on huge sheets of paper. He'd cover them with a secret smile when I came in. "'Ere Eg, yore'll see in due course." Due course! Where did Bag get words like that.

Ma said, "We gotta do our best fer Gran'pa. After all we owe everyfink to 'im." She gave me a pinch. "An' ter you." She explained about Bag's drawings. "'E's doin' the whatchmacallit, the deecor for the club. It's a secret."

Charlie kept himself to himself. He was writing. Not words because he couldn't read or write, but music. And from what I heard he was good and getting better. That left Freddie. I didn't see Freddie until band practice. This took place at dawn. The night before I'd said to Ma, "What about Freddie?"

"'Im," she said grimly. "'Im. 'E's a dead loss. Won't do nuffink. We just 'ave to keep 'im 'appy on the stuff, know what I mean. 'E's on cloud nine most of the time. But we need 'im for the band and when it's time for that we wheel 'im out and 'e does his fing."

And they did, and so did he. He was out of his face but he played the sax like a dream. Afterwards they gave him another glass of blood and put him back in his room to burble away quietly. Ma said, "It's sad reelly. I'm almost glad Pa ain't 'ere ter see it." Then she brightened up and said, "Well I suppose one out of four ain't that bad."

And what of his lordship? I saw a lot of him. I'd have breakfast in his room and we'd chat.
"Have you seen Vladimir," he said.
"Once," I replied. "In the street. He ignored me."
His lordship nodded sadly. "Poor Vladimir is a little, shall I say, narrow minded. He finds it difficult to change. That's a bad thing if you live a long time. Times change and we must change with them." Then he said, "Vladimir isn't going to like our plans here, not at all. Still, if he doesn't know he can't worry about it."
"I won't tell him," I replied.

Another day I was looking through his lordship's books. One looked particularly old. I took it out and saw an inscription in Latin inside the cover. I was never any good at Latin but I knew it said the book belonged to someone and then there was a long name. At the end of this was one word I was very

155

familiar with. I slammed the book shut and put it back in the bookcase quickly.

His lordship looked up from his bacon and eggs. "Why so much hurry my dear friend?" and he got up and joined me. In my haste to replace the book I'd pushed it in past the others so he could see which one it was. He pulled the book out, looked inside the cover and frowned. "I thought I'd got rid of all those," he said. He returned to his seat and patted the one by it to signal me to sit by him.

"We had to change the family name in about 1900," he said. I had a cousin, a dreadful bounder. He had no discretion, you would say he had a big mouth, a very common fellow who kept the company of actors and writers. Well he became friendly with a so-called writer, a Mr Bram Stoker and, one night, when he was intoxicated, out of his skull Mrs Scurf would say, he betrayed all our secrets, spilled the beans. This wretched writer fellow put a lot of it in a book. So we had to change our name. I'd say I'd never forgive my cousin but it would be pointless since someone who read the book got to him first. He was an exhibitionist. I always said sleeping in a coffin was asking for trouble and so it was and serve him right."

I looked at the ring on my finger, the one his lordship had given me. "So this is the crest of the Dracula family?"
"It is, it is, my dear boy," he said. "We were an ancient family and although it's true that some of my

ancestors were a little cruel I think it's sad we should be made such a mockery in the modern media."

I had some good chats with Boris. I said, "Isn't his lordship sad about Big Drac, I mean Vladimir."
"Yes," he said. "But the problem lies a long time ago I'm afraid. His lordship hasn't had a great deal of luck with his family."
"But he has friends," I said.
"A few," said Boris. "Friends come and go when you live this long."
"And enemies?" I said.
"Unfortunately enemies seem to last longer," he said.
"I would have thought his lordship had outlived all his enemies," I said.
"Not those of our blood," he said. "There's one left, a bad one."
"Who's he," I said.
"Count Arshog," said Boris.
Count Arshog it seemed was a really nasty bloke with size fourteen teeth and a temper to match.
"We and they had a few battles," said Boris, "until the countryside turned against us. That was unexpected, but that's democracy for you I suppose. Arshog was forced to leave first and he always blamed his lordship for it. Arshog was a good swordsman, the only man I've ever seen fight Igor to a standstill."
"What about his lordship?" I asked.
Boris smiled. "No one has ever beaten him, but then he and Arshog have never fought hand to hand. It's too late now, we'll never find out."

157

We also talked about Josh. "I knew his great grandfather quite well," Boris said. "Good in a fight, a superb swordsman and a good shot with the musket. But he was unreliable and I'm afraid it runs in the family. The grandfather grew up with Vladimir and wouldn't pay the respect Vladimir thought was due to him, so they didn't get on. And he got into a lot of trouble when he was young. He was also a spendthrift and by the time Josh's father came along the family was poor. That didn't stop Josh's father being even wilder and you know what happened to him." Boris pursed his lips and then smiled and said, "I think his lordship has your brother under control."

"Have you had to put him in the dungeon?" I asked. But he didn't say.

Please don't think I didn't spend time with Josh for I did. He was really into the music. He'd started singing and had quite a high voice, a bit like Michael Jackson. With his lordship sounding like Rod Stewart and Sandra a bit like Madonna they really put some numbers on. I said I'd heard a lot worse on the top twenty. Ma said, "You just wait kiddo, we're gonna knock 'em fer six."

I stayed three weeks. On my last day Ma said, "We gonna make a go of this Eg." Then she said, "Yore very fond of Gran'pa ain't yer." After a bit she added, "'E's very 'ansom for such an old geezer ain't 'e."

Later when I was talking to his lordship he said, "Mary" (Mrs. Scurf) is a woman of great sense and determination and a real business woman." I

158

nodded and he added, "She's really quite a good looking woman, quite reminds me of a great aunt of mine. Mind you that one had unpleasant habits, you know the sort of thing, chopping heads off and so on, I never did agree with it. That's man's work." He shook his head. "She married an enemy of the family. She's still alive I understand, but I haven't seen her for a hundred years."

He was lost in thought for a moment. Then he brightened up and said, "Mary has really taken to the language. I'm going to teach her French next, that will suit her."

Later that evening his lordship drove me to the airport. "We'll see you next holiday," he said. "Just before the opening. We'll have some more surprises for you."

CHAPTER 2

On my return I found Dad had opened a new office. Not only that, but at home the house rang to familiar tunes. Beethoven? No. To the Scurfs and Josh and his lordship.

"Not my cup of tea," said Dad, "but it's good." He looked very thoughtful. This was unlike Dad, who usually stomped round the house when we had our music on loud, muttering things like "...can't think ....no peace in my own home .... ruddy row ..." and so on." Still, as they say, if it's your own you don't mind it so much.

Josh still rang every Friday, but I could see or rather hear that his heart wasn't in it, and that he was only really interested in what was going on over there. I asked him how the decorating of the club was going. "Can't say anything Eg," he said. "It's a big secret but it'll blow your mind when you see it."

About four weeks before the end of the next term I got a letter from Ma. It was written in French. It took me some time to translate it (with a bit of help). I will say that Ma, like Josh, had a natural gift for languages. She hadn't learned English very well but these new ones were quite different.

I spent a bit of time writing the translation out and have tried to keep the flavour of it. It went as follows:

"My dear Eg,

You will see that my dear lordship has started to teach me French and since I find that already I speak and indeed think in it better than in English I therefore use it to write to you. I feel sure that as an intelligent young man you will have no difficulty in understanding my hesitating sentences in this new language."

You must be joking I thought. What's the French for gobsmacked. She continued,

"I am writing because his lordship has asked me to marry him and we both wanted you to be the first to know. I suppose it could be said that your brother Josh brought us together but we see it as being you. And, undoubtedly, but for you I would not have been alive to meet his lordship, let alone to accept his proposal."

That was generous I thought. It had been a close thing and really I blew it. On the other hand, if I'd called the police Ma might have been writing to me from the zoo. The letter continued,

"When it comes to wedding presents his lordship and I" (this was all a bit grand I thought) "have everything we need" (Ma had certainly hit the jackpot). "In view of that we have decided to change the usual arrangement and instead give presents to our special friends of whom you are the dearest."

That was very nice, although it did occur to me that they didn't have any other friends. I read on as follows.

161

"You may not be aware, since we instructed the agents not to tell you, but our old house was taken off the market, and it is that house that we wish to give you as a present. I have spoken to the children about it and they all agree. His lordship has been most generous to all of us, and we feel that you should share it."

"So we ask you to go to the lawyers in your town whom your father employs and they will deal with the matter."

At this point the French, I am pleased to say, ended and Ma finished the letter in English as follows.

"Dere Eg, I ant too good in English but wot I want ter sai is that the kids and me reelly apprechiatte wot you done.
Love Ma, xxx
P.S Grandpa sends his love too."

I phoned Ma. "You deserve it, Eg" she said. "It's wot we want. We've landed wiv our bums in the butter 'ere."

The second letter came a week before my flight and it was from Josh.

"Dear Eg,
Just a short note enclosing some of the advertising for the Club. Isn't it wicked! You can see why it was a secret! We open in two weeks.
Love, Josh.
P.S. I've sent a copy to Big Drac. He'll be gutted!"

162

Big Drac was indeed gutted. We and he had steered very clear of one another but the next day I bumped into him. He must have lain in wait for me. He had the leaflets in his hand and was he pissed off. He caught me by the shoulder and waved the papers at me.

"What do you know about this?" he shouted.

"Nothing," I said. "I got them in the post yesterday myself." For a moment I thought he was going to attack me. His eyes looked wild. Then he let me go suddenly. "It can't be allowed," he said. "The old man has gone off his head. He'll have to be stopped." And he turned abruptly and walked away.

I looked at the leaflet. "Come to the Vampire's Den," it said. "11 p.m. until dawn. Grand Opening Soon."

CHAPTER 3

A week later I was sitting in the plane on my way back to brother Josh and his new family.

As usual it was a night flight. I was trying to doze, and let the seat down so I could lie back a bit. As I lay there I heard two quiet voices in the seats behind me. One said, "Arshog has been waiting for a chance like this for two hundred years."

I froze, scarcely breathing in case I might miss hearing their words. The other one said, "The son's got it in for him. Mind, I see his point, they can't be allowed to get away with this, it will cause trouble for all of us."

The first man spoke again. "He tried his own people but they wouldn't help. That's why he came to Arshog."

His companion said, "He may regret it. Arshog has a way with traitors when they've served his purpose."

A long silence followed. Then one of them said, "What time do we do it?"

The other replied, "Tomorrow, at eight in the evening."

Then there was another long silence. I held my breath until I thought I would suffocate. The first one said, "Six of us should be enough, especially if we surprise them."

There was no more, not that I heard. After about fifteen minutes I got up and went to the loo. I looked at them as I passed. They were both asleep. They looked old and tough. One was bald and the other

164

had a horrid scar on his forehead. They had the vampire look.

I was the first out of that plane and I didn't wait for my luggage. I threw myself into the Mercedes.
"What's the matter?" asked Boris.
"Arshog," I said. "Two men behind me talking about Arshog, one bald and one with a scar on his forehead. They'll be coming out in a minute."
"I know them," said Boris, and I told him what I'd overheard.

When we arrived, his lordship was very thoughtful. Then he said, "We have thirty six hours. We will discuss it further this evening. In the meantime my dear boy we must make you welcome."

I certainly had a welcome, and a guided tour as well. I didn't know whether to laugh or cry. The nightclub was fabulous, the fittings wonderful, the atmosphere terrific, but the theme! It was done up as a crypt with stone walls and dripping water and cobwebs and so on.
"Who on earth thought this up?" I gasped.
Josh said, "It was Bag actually. He's very artistic. He did all the layout and design. Really clever, isn't it."
"But it's crazy," I said "Crazy. You're asking for trouble." I was beginning to sound like Big Drac.
But Josh said, "That was Bag's idea too. He said it was perfect cover. If it's our trademark no one will believe it."
That sounded unlikely to me. I said, "What did his lordship say?"

165

Josh laughed. "He said it was time he lived a bit dangerously and that he'd forgotten what it was like."

Later I discussed it with Ma. "It's double or quits," she said. "Gran'pa 'as a certain reputation 'ere. If we want ter play we 'ave to 'ave publicity and if we 'ave publicity there's gonna be rumours. This way people won't believe it."
"And what if it goes wrong?"
"Then we 'ave ter move and start again" she said. "When yer've done it once it ain't so difficult. Gran'pa says 'e was getting fed up with 'ere anyway, leastways as it was. He wants ter 'ave a go."
I said, "You call him Grandpa but there was all this his lordship stuff in the letter."
She punched me in the arm, "Well, young Eg, it's like this init. Gran'pa's learned me good in French and it's different when I talk in that. In English I'm real common but in French I've learned it posh and I'm real posh. In English I'm Ma, but in French I'm a lady."

I wondered if life was so simple and decided that it might be, especially if you married someone with five wagon-loads of treasure.

CHAPTER 4

That evening we discussed the impending holocaust. I don't know why I was so worried. Over the centuries his lordship must have mastered all the arts of war, subtle plans, clever manoeuvres and so on.

And what was the master plan? So far as I could see it consisted of waiting for Arshog and his men to come through the front door and then to hack away with sabres. Very subtle. Maybe I'd missed something.
"I suppose they'll knock first," I said.
Boris and his lordship just smiled.

Afterwards I felt pretty gloomy I can tell you. What did you do on holiday? Oh I went to a battle, nothing special, just swords and sabres and a load of vampires. Terrific.

But his lordship, Boris and Levin were really enjoying it, rushing around like young boys with smiles on their faces. "I haven't had so much fun in years," said Boris. Well, I suppose it wouldn't do if we all liked the same thing, but some people have very odd tastes I must say.
"Suppose they come in with machine guns and zap us all?" I said.
Boris laughed, "That's not Arshog's style. Boiling oil perhaps."
"Levin's very quiet isn't he," I said. "He just keeps grinning."

"Arshog captured him once, in an ambush" said Boris. "Sent him back with a written message for his lordship. It had to be written because Arshog first cut out Levin's tongue. We don't usually talk about it because that upsets Levin. He's smiling because he's thinking about what he's going to do to Arshog."

First catch your chicken I thought. Mr. Arshog sounded a charming gentleman. I thought back to the good old days when I only had to worry about spots and the Scurfs.

This was crazy. Later I found Boris in the kitchen sharpening half a dozen sabres. He was whistling and licking his lips.

"I've been thinking about these machine guns," I said.

"Don't worry Mr. Egbert. Arshog wouldn't do anything like that."

"That's not what I meant," I said and I came out with it. "What I mean is, well, why don't we get a gun or two. I mean, this is barbaric," and I pointed at the sabres.

Boris got quite annoyed. "His lordship is a gentleman and so for all his faults is Count Arshog. They'd never behave like that. Guns! Really, I've never heard such a suggestion."

I could see I was getting nowhere but I tried again. "Wouldn't it be sensible to get more help? If there are a lot more of us than of them we'd be bound to win."

Boris raised an eyebrow. "If something like that got out we'd never be able to hold up our heads again."

I wasn't too worried about holding up my head. Holding on to it was the problem.

Mum rang later. "Hello darling" she said. "How are you?"
"Fine Mum. Everything is fine."
Ignorance is bliss. Why worry the old folks unnecessarily.
"Is it hot darling?"
Getting hotter by the hour.
"Make sure you have a good rest my pet," she said.
Longer than you may think, I thought. Rest in peace: in pieces more like. I put the phone down. Be a brave boy, Eg, I said to myself. It made 'A' levels seem like a doss.

Not that I was expected to fight. His lordship was quite firm. "All of you are to stay locked in the Club," he said.

All right if we won. But otherwise? Arshog might be a gentleman but he might also have old-fashioned ideas about looting and pillage. I didn't fancy finding out.

Nor did Ma, and she summoned us lot to her own council of war. "I ain't gonna sit 'ere like a turkey waitin' fer Christmas. And I ain't gonna be a widder twice in one year," she said grimly. "We need a plan," she added.
"Ain't Gran'pa got one?" asked Sandra.

"'E's got the plan for the Battle of 'astings wivout the arrows" Ma replied. "Says these fings 'ave ter be done proper. Proper mess, more like, if you ask me."

And with that, Ma led us to the utility room, where his lordship seldom came. The floor was covered in scrap metal. She picked up something that looked like a large pineapple with spikes and gave it to Bag. "Wot's that Ma?" he asked.
"Just somefink wot I found in the cellar," she replied, and picked up another rusted piece.
You couldn't mistake what that was. She whirled the battle-axe round her head.
"The Scurfs don't get left out of nuffink," she said.

Ma was right. And she got me thinking. I made my own plans and went shopping. I found an oriental grocers in a side street and made my purchase there. Then I bought a water pistol. I returned to my room and made my own preparations for battle.

CHAPTER 5

They arrived at eight on the dot in two expensive cars with tinted windows like something from an American gangster film. I don't think his lordship was the only one who'd left his old home with a few wagon-loads of treasure.

Arshog looked very fierce when he got out. He wore a studded leather cap and body armour. His face was white and his lips red. His merry men looked as bad. I wondered if we'd been caught in a time warp.

I was looking out of an upper window from the gallery over the hall. I expect you think they leapt out of the car and rushed into the house. No, they didn't. They climbed out and dusted themselves down. Then they went to the boot of one car and took out the weapons. Arshog's sword was huge. He leaned on it like a walking stick. Then they had a chat. Then they walked to the front door. These vampires had a strange way of going to war.

Looking over the stairway I saw Boris go to the door in full fighting kit, chain mail and helmet, his sabre in his hand. I heard what must be Arshog's voice.
"You're expecting us then."
There was a long silence. I didn't care to think what would have happened if Boris had just been in his butler's outfit.
"Do come in," he said.
They did. All together and very noisily, waving a lot of sharp hardware. But they weren't concentrating. They didn't notice Levin and his lordship behind the

171

door, I saw his lordship get one of them. That shortened the odds a bit.

Then, for a moment, they all stood still. "I see you've brought that agricultural implement of yours," said his lordship. "Why don't you get a gentleman's weapon?"

Arshog curled his lip. "This is a weapon for killing peasants and that's what we're going to do today." He looked at Levin and said, "When I cut out your tongue I threw away the wrong bit." That wasn't a very nice thing to say, was it. Up came the swords and they were at it again.

I expect you think this is all very exciting. Well, it may be to read about but I can tell you it wasn't my idea of a good holiday. I tiptoed to the back stairs and then ran to the Club, where I reported to Ma. As I ran I could hear lots of clanging behind me.

Left to myself I think I would have gone for help, possibly at the airport before I caught a plane. But not Ma. She'd have made a good general for the ancient Britons.

"Sandra, 'ave you oiled that fing proper" she said as I entered. Sandra wore a chain mail shirt hanging off one shoulder and reaching to her ankles. She was fiddling with a cross bow.

"'Ere Ma, look at this". That was Bag. He was in a brown leather jacket studded with metal and was throwing his spiked club in the air and catching it as it turned over. He looked at me as I came in.

"Cool man," he said.

172

Suit yourself, I thought. I didn't feel cool at all. Hot and sweaty and ready to run away.

"Right," said Ma after I'd told her what had happened. Then she looked over her shoulder and shouted, "Lay off Charlie". Charlie was experimenting with a ball and chain and was whirling round with it. He let it go and it flew off and stuck in the wall.

"'Ere," said Ma. "'Oo d'yer finks gonna mend that? 'Is lordship ain't made of money yer know."

Ma had her best purple dress on and all her jewellery.

"Shouldn't you be wearing armour Ma?" I said.

"I gotta look me best fer 'is lordship," she said, and put down her battle axe. "Now, young Eg. Get inter that". "That" was a suit of armour that must have been old when his lordship was a boy.

"It don't fit no one else," said Ma. "An' 'is lordship promised yer Ma 'e'd look after you. So get inside it."

It seemed Ma's idea of looking after me did not involve excluding me from the battle.

I got my top half into the armour but no more. Just as well, since the secret weapon was in the pocket of my jeans. Ma made me put the helmet on, which was a problem since the visor kept falling down so I couldn't see anything.

"'Ere," said Sandra. "Let me give you an 'and." And she sellotaped the visor up. We were ready to go.

173

CHAPTER 6

Out of the Club's front door we went, like refugees from a fancy dress party. As we approached the back of Arshog's car Bag said, "'Ere, there's someone in there." And there was. We sorted that out quickly and quietly. I wondered how we were going to explain it to his lordship.

We were at the front door now. Ma said, "On yer marks, get set, go," and in we rushed, Ma at the front whirling her battle axe and shrieking Scurf battle cries.

The battle froze for a minute. I could see we were needed. Another of Arshog's men lay in a corner so it was only four to three. But Boris looked cut about and Levin's left arm hung loosely. Only his lordship seemed untouched.

Arshog barked an order and two of his men turned on us. Arshog and the other bloke fought like fiends to keep his lordship Boris and Levin back. Not much hope of help from them I thought as the two vampire warriors bore down on us. It occurred to me that we were supposed to be doing the rescuing.

The one with the scar shouted horribly as he came towards us. But as he raised his sword, a little stick seemed to grow in the front of his neck. He stopped, just like that, and fell flat on his face. I heard Bag shout, "Good shot Sandra".
Comforting though this was, it still left the small problem of the other man, covered in armour and

blood, his red-lipped mouth wide open in battle cry and his sword high above his head, about to come down on Ma. She'd swiped at him with her battle axe and had missed and was sitting on the floor looking dazed.

It was clearly the time and place for Eg's secret weapon. I took the water pistol from my pocket and fired it right into the man's big, open, red mouth.

Now, if you dissolve a lot of garlic powder in water, put it in a water pistol and shoot it into a vampire's mouth it makes him very ill very quickly. While he was puking his guts out on the floor Charlie whacked him with his ball and chain.

I looked up just in time to see his lordship cut down the last of Arshog's men. Arshog stood surrounded. For a moment no one spoke or moved.

Then his lordship spoke. "My dear fellow," he said. "We've never had the chance to match our blades. Perhaps today we can find out who is the better swordsman. May I suggest you put down that vulgar weapon in your hand so that we can provide you with something more suitable for a person of your breeding."

Boris offered Arshog his sabre. Personally I thought Arshog's sword was just right for him.
"What are the terms?" growled Arshog.
"What you'd expect," said his lordship. "If you win you are free to go."

It took about half an hour. First one was winning and then the other. His lordship was very skilled and he was strong. But Arshog was like a tank and seemed tireless. The strange thing was that I think both of them were enjoying it. But I feared for his lordship for Arshog must in the end wear him down.

It only needed one mistake. But in the end it was Arshog who made it and he staggered back with his lordship's sabre deep in his side.

CHAPTER 7

Afterwards his lordship was very calm and business like. To Ma he said, "Thank you my dear. I don't think we could have managed without you. Is that my old battle axe? I thought I had got rid of it years ago." To me he said, "I'm not sure what you did but I suspect I am indebted to you yet again. You can explain it all to me later." To Sandra he said, "That was a good shot. Not very sporting, that's the sort of thing you shoot peasants with, but I think we'd bitten off more than we could chew. And it wasn't very sporting of Arshog to bring that sword." He added, "And we did hide behind the door didn't we." To Levin and Boris he said, "Drag Arshog next door and we'll do the business for him." Levin looked a very happy man. To the rest of us his lordship said, "Would you please go to the kitchen and wait for us."

Ma brewed up.
"Who's goin' ter tell Grandpa?" said Sandra.
Ma said firmly, "I fink Eg will do it best."
"Cuppa tea?" said Ma as his lordship finally arrived.
"A large blood and whisky," he said. He looked tired and I hated what I had to do.
I said, "There is one more thing."
He grunted.
I went on, "There's another one of them. We found him in the car. He's tied up."
His lordship wasn't too interested. He spoke to Boris. "Go and see to it Boris. Send him on his way. You know what to say."
I said, "It's Vladimir, your son."

177

His lordship's shoulders sagged. He got up slowly. "Come with me," he said to Boris, and they left the room. As he went out Ma gave him a hug and I heard Bag say, "I'm really sorry Grandpa. I 'ope we didn't 'urt him."

Later I heard his lordship say to Ma, "He didn't tell that wife of his. I suppose I must telephone her." And he did. He said, "I don't think you knew Vladimir had paid me a quick visit my dear ..... just business .... anyway he's a little unwell, and I think he should stay with us for a week or two."

We saw no more of Arshog and his men apart from one who survived. They let him go.
"It's for the best," said Boris. "It gets round that way. He'll talk about it. Makes it less likely we'll be bothered again."

His lordship gave the man a bag to take with him. It contained Arshog's head. I often wondered how the man got it through customs. Excuse me sir what's this? Just something I'm taking home for a friend.

I don't know where the others went. In the vegetable garden I daresay. I think Levin was very busy with his hammer and stakes. A few days afterwards I said to his lordship, "What about the police. I mean you can't just do people in like this."
"Who's going to complain dear boy," he said. "And where are the bodies?"
During his stay I probably saw more of Big Drac than anyone else did. That's because I took his food to him. Why I volunteered for this I'm not sure. I don't

like dungeons, and he ranted at me whenever I appeared, shaking his chains. But he was quieter after a couple of weeks there.

His lordship did a lot of telephoning and I think it was to Igor and the others who lived near Big Drac. I overhead one conversation. His lordship said, "If he gets out of line you have a free hand so far as I'm concerned Igor. Do whatever is necessary."

After the grand opening his lordship took Big Drac to the airport. He did not speak of him again.

CHAPTER 8

The opening of the Club was amazing. His lordship spent a deal of money on it. All the press were there. People were flown in from all over. I recognized a lot of famous faces.

Ma was magnificent. She only spoke in French. The Countess they called her and she looked it, in a red silk dress that cost a fortune and showed off this new figure she'd managed to get. She'd even stopped dribbling on her clothes.

Ma was imperious. Really. Like an Empress. I don't know how she did it. But to me and the rest, in English, she was just our Ma. "Cor they love it, don't they" she said. "Treat 'em like dirt, an' they lap it up."

The other Scurfs loved it too. They all loved it, dressed up as vampires. But I think Boris was the one who enjoyed it most. He was the doorman and bouncer and from time to time he would leap out and pretend to bite the guests as they came in. "Wonderful!" he said to me afterwards. "After all this time hiding. You can have no idea how wonderful it is."

His lordship had insisted on one precaution, that they all wore fake vampire teeth. "We can't have any unfortunate accidents, and you can take them out when you play," he said.

Freddie was a bit of a problem. Being out of his head most of the time his tooth control wasn't what it might be so they stuck him in the back row when the time came to play.

Did it go down well? I don't need to tell you, for you know. It was a riot. The band stood there in their vampire costumes and then Ma and his lordship came on. Ma was a wow and the audience cheered her as she settled herself down behind the drums, but it was when the singing started that the audience really got going. And they rose to their feet when his lordship, Sandra and Josh sang Charlie and Joshs' latest number.

Bag put his fitness training to good use and when he wasn't playing, danced round the stage, leaping, break-dancing, doing back-flips, everything.

After they finished playing and the disco started again, the champagne flowed. I saw one reporter trying to interview Ma. He tried to speak to her in English but she would only answer in French. "I do not understand ze English," she said to him, winking at me.

They was a nasty moment when Freddie decided he didn't want to go back to his room. But Levin dealt with that. Freddie wasn't in very good shape and wasn't in a position to object. I heard his lordship say to Ma, "I think we're going to have to do something about Freddie my dear."

We sat round this huge table, getting up, moving round, having a really good time, coming and going. I noticed Bag on the other side of the table. There was this good-looking bird next to him. She had the look all right, she'd be asking for a whisky and blood cocktail once the Club was closed.

It was difficult to tell her age but I could see she and Bag had really taken to one another. An older woman might do him good I thought. Later in the evening I found myself next to his lordship and I asked him about her.

"Ah, that's Katherine" he said. "A lovely girl, very clever, very artistic, she's always had a thing about young men you know."

"Always," I thought. "Always" was a long time for his lordship. "Is she related to you then?" I asked.

"Oh yes," he replied. "One of my favourite nieces. Amazing how she keeps herself like that."

Amazing indeed. I wondered whether to tell Bag that this bird he was lusting over was more than one hundred years old, but what was the point. I mean if he couldn't tell the difference it didn't matter did it. He'd find out, but how? My mind boggled when I thought about it.

His lordship was in a very good mood. "I'll miss you when you go back dear boy. So will Mary, so will we all," he said. There was a silence while he seemed lost for words, something unusual for him. Then he said, "You know you could have a good life here, with us if you joined the family. There are a lot of advantages quite apart from living a long time."

"I don't think I'd be happy," I said, and we had a long silence within the noise round us. He patted me on the shoulder and said, "I'm sorry. I thought you'd say something like that. You don't mind my asking do you".

"No of course not," I said, and I didn't.

I looked at Josh. My little brother. Well, I didn't need to worry about looking after him. Sandra had clearly decided that was her job.

Ma was everywhere. On my way back from the loo I passed the office and put my head round the door. There was Ma on a flying visit. Punching buttons on the computer and clucking with approval with the figures that came up on the screen.

"'Ere, young Eg," she said. "We're going ter the bloomin' moon, all the way."

I didn't go to the moon. I went home. They all came to the airport to see me off.

CHAPTER 9

And we all lived happily ever after. For a bit. Everything went well. Tabitha, school, Mum and Dad, Dad's business, everything. As for news of Josh and the Scurfs and his lordship, there was no shortage of that. In letters, on the television, in the papers. Yes, they'd cracked it. A record producer at the grand opening saw to that. Five number ones in a year. Anyway, I expect you saw that article in *Hello.*

Josh got very friendly with Sandra, and Sandra was keen on Josh keeping up with his education. Ma said it was good publicity. I don't suppose you want to know about Freddie. Nobody wanted to know about Freddie and I'm not surprised. They had a lot of trouble with him. His teeth kept on hanging out when he wasn't playing. It didn't matter at first but it was different when they put out their DVDs, with close-ups and so on, so they had to send Freddie to a vampire dentist. Goodbye teeth.

Dad was really mellow. He'd keep saying things like how hard Josh would have to work to spend his copyright money. It didn't take long for him to become international agent for the group. He was really into it. His hair was even longer. And the clothes! It was really embarrassing. But he was happy and there was lots of dosh. And Mum didn't have to work so hard so it was alright really. Tabitha and I talked about it all. Not all, of course. There was a world I couldn't share with her. Not yet.

As for Big Drac, I didn't think much of him in either sense. And I daresay I was wrong in both ways. But I didn't think he mattered any more. I had heard Mrs. Drac had left him and taken Little Drac with her. Josh told me that and I suppose he got it from his lordship. Big Drac could stew on his own.

I passed his house several times. The gates were chained up and a big sign on them said "Keep out". There was a shop down the road and once I stopped there.

"Is that big house with the gates for sale" I said.

"'Im" said the shopkeeper. "No, 'e's a queer one. Off 'is trolley if you ask me. Always was a funny lot that but since 'is wife left, well, 'e's round the bend if you ask me."

This shopkeeper was a good judge of character as I found out. I'd finished my exams. Tabitha and I were in the supermarket just before closing time. We were in the far corner of a empty aisle when I saw Big Drac, pushing a full trolley.

I knew there was going to be trouble. I just felt it. We were in the sauces and spices section and I had an idea as he bore down on us. The old ideas are the best ones. I took a tube of garlic puree from the shelf.

He was a big man and did he look frightening. His hair was greased back and his face dead white. He was in an old fashioned black suit, stained and fraying. His shirt had no collar and he was unshaven. But what were really gross were his eyes which were wild and mad, and his mouth which was red and snarling.

"What on earth is that?" whispered Tabitha clutching my arm.

Big Drac pushed the trolley towards us hemming us in. I noticed it was full to the top with bottles of whisky, packets of raw meat and tins of dog food.

He leaned over the trolley. "You nasty little creep," he said. "You've ruined my life. I'll fix you. And when I've fixed you I'll fix the rest of them." He smelt of whisky.

He looked at Tabitha. "This is your little friend, eh?" he said. "You wouldn't like anything to happen to her, eh?" He pulled her towards him. "She looks very tasty to me," he said and opened his mouth. I'm all for letting it all hang out but this was ridiculous.

I really wasn't prepared for this. I mean when you go down the supermarket for some soy sauce and crisps you don't expect to be attacked by a vampire do you.

And what did Eg do? Run away? No, we were cornered. Call for help? Strange as it may seem I didn't think of that. But you know what I did. I undid the top of my trusty tube of garlic and squirted it into his open mouth.

Splodge, right past his huge yellow fangs and down the hatch. But not down for long. Back he staggered and up it all came. All over the frozen chickens. The supermarket staff weren't pleased, but I don't think Big Drac noticed. We left quietly.

I will say, I was really impressed by Tabitha. Not a scream. Not even a squeak. But as we left the supermarket she said, "And what the hell was that. Jaws?"

I could see she wasn't going to be satisfied with any old story. So I told her the truth. She found it difficult to believe at first. But she'd seen Big Drac's teeth slide out, and so many other things in the past slid into place.

"Now I see it," she kept saying. We sat up really late talking about it. The next day I bought us both little water pistols and filled them with garlic water.

CHAPTER 10

For a few weeks we were really edgy. Several times Tabitha thought she saw Big Drac following her. Once I could have sworn I saw his car pass our house at night.

As for Josh, just when I was looking forward to taking Tabitha on my next trip to see him he rang and announced he was coming back. Not just him but all of them. And not back home. No, back to a rented ancient monument fit for a family of pop stars. And with a cellar full of bottles of blood and no mirrors. I wondered if it was a good idea.

"His lordship says the natives are getting restless here," Josh said to me over the phone. "A gang of locals turned up with sharpened stakes. We treated it as a joke, but his lordship says it's time to move on."

I looked forward to them coming back. In the meantime, I had a lot of study to do. I did much of my work at the Scurfs' old home and sometimes I'd stay there overnight. And that was when it happened.

I woke suddenly. I didn't know why, but then I heard the noise in the next room. Someone was in there and not being very quiet either. I wondered if the Scurfs had come back early.

I didn't need much brain power to realise it couldn't be that. Perhaps it was a burglar. I thought of shouting out an invitation to take whatever he wanted. Then it occurred to me that I might be on the list, and that it might be Big Drac. I thought of how to protect myself. I considered pretending I hadn't heard anything. Maybe It would go away.

But perhaps It was going to come into the bedroom and do me in in my own bed. Out I got as quickly as the thought. I stood and shook by the door. As It charged in, I would nip out.

You will be surprised that this plan went like clockwork. I could hear snuffling outside the door. I couldn't recall Big Drac snuffling but maybe he had a cold. Next, the door was flung open and a huge black shape rushed past and onto the bed. There was a lot of unpleasant thumping.

Out I went through the door like a rocket. But as I got half way across the living room I realised that I'd heard a most unexpected sound. It was weeping: great big heavy sobs. That didn't sound like Big Drac, and as I reached the safety of the other side of the living room I turned the light on. I took a carving knife from the dresser door and advanced to the bedroom door.

There on the bed was a shambling untidy man in clothes that looked as if they'd come from a jumble sale. His hands were over his head and he was crying.

I turned the light on. What a sight. He looked at me. Was he ugly! He shrank away.

"I dun wrong," he said. "I din' do you in. The big man going to hurt me now." He put his thumb in his mouth awkwardly and continued to cry. Yes, I'd met Frank.

CHAPTER 11

I can't say I felt very friendly towards my visitor. But it wasn't very long before I felt really sorry for him. He was a real mess.

He looked as if he'd been in a dreadful accident, for he was horribly scarred. There was a red scar stitched right round his neck and the same round his wrists. And his right hand was on back to front which made sucking his thumb very awkward.

"What's your name?" I asked.

"Thing's my name," he replied. "That's what the big man calls me," and he started to cry again. This was really weird. He must have been nearly 2 metres tall, and big, but he talked like a kid and seemed as simple as a baby. I found him a hanky.

"Who's the big man?" I asked. But I knew the answer already.

"He's tall an' black, wiv funny teeth an' he hurts me if I don't do what he wants."

"And did he do those scars to you?" I asked. It blew his nose. The sound echoed round the room.

"Yeth," he said. "When he put me together."

All of a sudden I realised. It was man-made, put together by Big Drac, to do his will.

Looking at this pathetic thing I could see a great danger ahead.

"You must go," I said. "Right now".

He got off the bed and knelt at my feet.

"Plees don't send me back to him, plees" he begged.

I couldn't bear it. I had not got rid of Josh and the vampires to get lumbered with a monster. But he who hesitates is lost. That's what my Mum says and

191

she's quite right. I hesitated. Then I said, "You need a proper name. I'm going to call you Frank."

He stopped crying for a moment and a little smile touched his ugly face.

"That's a nice name," he said. "I prefer it to Thing."

I looked at the ruins of my bed. The duvet was slashed and leaking feathers. Better than blood, I suppose. A nasty looking machete lay on top. It really freaked me out. But Frank was clearly unsuited to this sort of work. He saw me looking.

"He made me do it," he said. "I din' want to."

I could see that Big Drac's Frankenstein programme had not been a total success.

"How did you get in?" I asked.

Frank wiped his slobbery nose with the back of his hand. "The big man did the back door," he said.

More expense I thought. Then I had a horrible thought. Had big Drac tasted the goods. I mean had he sent out an ordinary monster or a blood sucking one. I sat Frank in an arm chair. "I'll get us a cup of tea," I said but I got a bit more than that. In the kitchen I pricked my finger and put the blood on a saucer. When I waved it under his nose Frank's brown stumpy teeth stayed where they were I'm pleased to say. So it could have been worse.

I was watching Frank dribbling his cup of tea down his chin and over his clothes when I had another dreadful thought. We were not alone. Somewhere, outside, was Big Drac, waiting for his monster to return.

Off I went, like a cat chased by a dog in a cartoon. I checked the windows and the front door. Then the back door. Big Drac had forced the lock, and I hadn't used the bolts. Now I pushed them firmly across . There were plenty of bolts thank goodness. Actually it wasn't goodness that I had to thank but the bailiffs, debt collectors and angry neighbours of the Scurfs.

Snug as a bug in a rug, or possibly a rat in a trap, I returned to Frank. He was sitting on the edge of the chair looking frightened.
"You won't let him get me Mister, will you?" he said.
"You'd better call me Eg," I replied.
"I'll be your best friend," he said.
Great. At least I had Frank on my side! I heard the back door rattle and thought of ignoring it.
"It's him," said Frank. "The big man." He whimpered and moaned and tried to hide behind the settee. But his backside stuck out.

I was beginning to see things from Big Drac's point of view. There's not much point in having a monster at your disposal if it isn't prepared to do a bit of monstering. I left Frank to his thumb and the settee, found a bucket, filled it and went upstairs. I opened the window and looked out. Underneath I saw a familiar shape by the back door.
"What are you doing?" I said.
He looked up. I'm sure he stamped his foot.
"Where is he?" he said in a slurred voice.
"Who?" I replied.
He didn't like that. "You know who," he said and kicked the door.
"You're trespassing," I said as I poured the bucket of water over him. He liked that even less. Then he

smashed a window in. I saw it all in my mind's eye. He'd get in, and first he'd suck all my blood out, and then he'd pull Frank to bits.

I looked at the bucket. None of your plastic buckets for the Scurfs. This was a heavy, dented, galvanised steel job rescued from some scrap yard. There was a lot of grunting and swearing going on down below and I threw the bucket towards it as hard as I could. I heard a thud and the cursing stopped.

I couldn't leave Big Drac lying outside the house. People might think the Scurfs had returned. But I couldn't carry him myself. I had a dreadful job persuading Frank to help. We left Big Drac in his car, and made a quick getaway

But where were we going to get away to? Not the Scurfs. Big Drac might come back for more. No, we had to go home.

CHAPTER 12

You would think that after all that fuss about Josh I'd find it easy to tell my parents that I'd invited a monster to stay. I mean, it didn't really affect them did it. Not like Josh. Not like being told your son was a vampire.

But, somehow, the words didn't come easily when I went downstairs in the morning. Maybe I was just tired. We'd crept in quietly, or as quietly as Frank could be. Being quiet wasn't his strong point. And I'd set my alarm so I'd be up early to explain.

You've done it all before Eg, I thought as I swallowed my cornflakes. I rehearsed in my head. I've made a new friend Mum, well actually bits of several new friends. Or, isn't it amazing what medical science can do now... Or, do you believe in life after death Dad?
In the end I said, "Big Drac's been at it again."
That didn't get much reaction.
"At what dear?" said Mum.
"He's made a monster," I said.
"He certainly is dear," Mum replied.
"No," I said. "He's really made a monster. A human monster like Frankenstein, made out of bodies."
"Don't be daft," said Dad. "You've been watching too many videos." He stared hard at me. "You haven't been taking anything have you?"
"No," I replied indignantly. "And it's true."
"Huh, I'll believe it when I see it," said Dad, disappearing behind his paper.

195

"It's true and you can see. He's upstairs in the spare room." The paper sort of froze. Then it gradually came down. Behind it Dad had a bad case of bulging eyes.

"What did you say?"

"He's a very nice monster," I said. "Very polite and not at all fierce. Like a baby really. He doesn't look very good but he's got a great personality. You'll like him."

"Let's get it straight young man," said Dad. Oh dear, we were in for trouble. "Now, you met this monster yesterday evening and asked him to stay the night?"

"Well I suppose so, but it's very complicated," I replied.

"Huh," said Dad and turned towards Mum. "I think he'd better go and see the Doctor. And I think I'd better go and inspect the spare room."

We listened to his steps clumping up the stairs and then to them rattling down.

"There's a ruddy monster in the bed," he said to Mum. He turned to me. "Why didn't you tell us?" Dad seemed to have strong views on uninvited guests and he went on for a bit.

"Just because we've got a vampire in the family doesn't mean it's open house for any sort of weirdo or monster."

He was pacing up and down. He'll start pulling his hair in a minute I thought, and so he did.

"You'll be getting a werewolf for a pet next," he said.

I said nothing. With my luck he could be right.

When Dad's motor seemed to be running down Mum took over. "You'd better go and get him up, darling. Show him where the bathroom is and get him a clean towel. Then we can meet him."

196

Dad was looking down at the table muttering. I could hear a few phrases "....no peace ... all over again ... freaks ... zoo ... can't call your home your own ..."

Frank had pulled the duvet over his head and his feet stuck out at the bottom. I'd been relieved he didn't have a bolt through his neck. Now I saw he had one right through his left leg. Poor old Frank hadn't been put together very well.

I pulled the duvet back a little. Frank's bloodshot eyes were wide open.
"A man come in," he said. "I don' think he likes me."
"Oh, but he does," I said.
"Reelly?"
"He's my Dad. He's just a bit grumpy first thing". And when he finds monsters in the spare bedroom.
"I've run a bath for you," I said, for he was grubby. In fact, he smelled. The kindest thing you could say about him was that he didn't seem very well cared for.

Frank had never had a bath before and he loved it. He played with the soap and when I gave him a rubber duck left over from Josh's babyhood he was in ecstasy. "This is lovely," he said. "It like heaven. All warm and cosy." I asked how big Drac had kept him clean.
"He done me outside wiv the hose" he said.

Frank's clothes looked pretty horrible so I thought I'd better take them down to be washed. At the top of

197

the stairs I had a nasty thought. Perhaps Big Drac had glued him together and the hot water would dissolve it all. I had a picture of opening the bathroom door and seeing all the bits floating round one another. But when I went back he was playing with the duck and gurgling happily and nothing had fallen off. So I thought it would probably be all right.

I got one of Dad's dressing gowns and some slippers and pyjamas. I thought it would make Frank more presentable but it didn't work very well. He was a lot taller than Dad and the trousers were too short so you could see the bolt in his leg. I noticed he limped slightly.

"Does that trouble you," I asked.

"It's good isn't it," said Frank. "The big man said it was extra special. Not everyone has got one like that."

He was right.

He started to suck his thumb. It was sad. He had to twist his hand right round.

"Why did he put your hand on back to front" I asked.

"I dunno," said Frank. "It was the last bit. He did it when I was there."

This was really gross.

"He din' do it proper," Frank continued. "He was fallin' down an' swallowing that smelly stuff. Afterwards he said it din' matter cos it was only a second hand an' then he laughed an' fell down again." He sniffed sadly and added, "I tried sucking the other one but it don't taste the same as this one."

It was time to meet the family. I'd given Frank a shave and combed his hair. But you couldn't get

198

round the fact that he didn't seem to fit together properly. His arms were too long for his body and I'll swear one leg was shorter than the other. I looked at his face. He looked about thirty, with black hair, bushy eyebrows and a hooked nose. Big Drac hadn't been too fussy about his materials but then I suppose it hadn't been easy to get the parts.

"Where did the big man get, er the er, ...you. I mean ..the bits?" I said. I felt awkward. It seemed a rude question but Frank didn't mind.

"I dunno," he said. "He din tell me". He sniffed and wiped his nose. "He said sumfink about pigs. He said he couldn't get no good bits and couldn't make no silk purse out of a pig's ear." He pointed to his ear. "That in't a pig ear, Eg, is it?" He shook his head in puzzlement.

Mum and Dad were still at the breakfast table, pretending to eat. I introduced Frank to Dad.

"Hello Mister" said Frank. "Fank you for having me. That's a very good barf fing you got." He added "I never had no barf before".

Dad struggled to drag his eyes from the bolt in Frank's ankle. "Er, er, Frank, well, er, it's very nice to meet you," he said and sat down.

I looked at Frank with new eyes. Dad speechless, that was really something. He sat there staring at the scar round Frank's neck.

"Would you like breakfast?" Mum said.

I have to say that breakfast was not a great success. Frank's upbringing left something to be desired. First he picked all the cereal out of his bowl and ate it with his fingers, and then he put the bowl on the floor, got on his knees and licked the milk up. "You've got a very clean floor here Mrs," he said. "I reelly like living here."

CHAPTER 13

I was looking at the fixed smile on Dad's face wondering when it would crack when there was a knock on the door and Tabitha came in in a hurry.

"Someone's burgled your house," she said. "They broke a window".

"I know," I said. "Big Drac did it. Meet Frank."

Tabitha shook Frank's hand so vigorously I was worried it might come off. The shake slowed down as she noticed the scars there. Her eye travelled down to the bolt in his ankle and then up to the scar round his neck.

"Would you like to watch television Frank?" I said.

With Frank safely in front of the cartoons I explained it all briefly to Tabitha. By the time I'd finished Dad's voice had come back.

"He can't stay here. Anyway it's not natural. He's dead."

"He looks alive enough to me," said Tabitha. "I think he's rather sweet."

Tabitha was good at standing up for herself but it was the first time I'd seen her take on Dad. I was surprised. So was he. But not for long.

"I'm off on for a trip today," he said. "I've got a deal to do for the group. I'll be back in two days. When I return I do not expect to find any Martians or monsters here. Do I make myself clear?"

"Of course you do darling," said Mum. "Now you get yourself ready, and Eg and Tabitha will clear up."

And so Dad copped out, Mum pacified, and I wondered what on earth to do.

"You can't send him back to Big Drac," said Tabitha. "That's cruel. And he might get taught to be a proper monster, and then where would you be?"
She was right. Frank was safer where he was.

Later we took him shopping down the supermarket. That really got him excited. He was dancing at the other end of the aisle. It was so embarrassing, but what with Josh I'd got used to that sort of thing.
"Eg! Eg!" he shouted. "Come here. I dun found my food." And he had. Dog food. He clasped a tin to his chest, a big smile on his face. "It's reely good," he said. "You should try it."

I asked Frank to carry the shopping back but he said, "I dun my arm. Carrying the big man." He seemed really upset and I thought he'd start crying again so I carried the shopping myself.
"You're a good man," said Tabitha.
But I wondered how I always managed to get myself stuck with it. What was I going to do with Frank? I thought I'd sleep on it. When I got up I was no nearer to an answer. I was nearer to Dad's return though. But then my old friend Fate took a hand.

Mum was out and Frank was watching childrens' television when the doorbell rang. I opened it and there stood an old lady, stooping, in a Salvation Army uniform. She waved a collecting box at me. "Help us help the unfortunate," she said.

I thought of asking her for a contribution. I couldn't think of anyone more unfortunate than me. I

202

noticed she had thick makeup on and she was leaning on an umbrella.

I got some change and was putting it in the tin when she staggered and said, "Young man, I don't feel well. Do you think I could have a glass of water?"

I could feel my heart warming with the prospect of a nice easy good deed. So I gave the poor old thing my arm to the kitchen and sat her down at the table.

As I filled a glass at the sink I could see I had a bit of a problem. Not that I had eyes in the back of my head. But I did have a little mirror in front of me above the sink. And in that I saw an empty kitchen behind me.

It took a few seconds for the meaning of this to sink in and that wasn't a second too soon. As I turned around she was coming at me. Not a sweet old Salvation Army lady, but a snarling evil-faced vampire.

In front of her the umbrella was outstretched. This was no ordinary umbrella since it had a long sharp spike at the end. It was pointing straight at me.

Well, what do you do if you're attacked by an elderly Salvation Army lady. It's not easy to decide, especially if you've been brought up properly. Fortunately I had the presence of mind to sidestep sharply and grab the umbrella from her grasp as it went past.

My struggle over how to deal with this lapse of behaviour from an old age pensioner was resolved when she dug her nails in my face and kneed me in the groin. My blood was up! This should be easy, I thought as we fell to the ground. She can't be that old I said to myself as she threw me aside. Is this happening to me I pondered, as she rolled on to me and held me down. "Help!" I shouted, as she threw her head back and poked her teeth out like anti ballistic missiles.

Just before my jugular vein got nuked she took off. Up in the air. Am I dead, I thought. Is this what becoming a vampire is like? Then I noticed Frank. His face loomed over her. He was holding her at arms length and she was kicking and screaming abuse. "What's the nasty lady doing here, Eg?" he said.

I looked at her. Her makeup disguised the vampire look, until the teeth came out. Who was she? Had they taken over the local Salvation Army? I had a vision of a procession of uniformed vampires marching to a brass band.

She stopped shouting and fixed me with an evil look. "You're dead," she said. "Dead. You killed my Oggie. I'll get you if it's the last thing I do!" Who was Oggie? I didn't know. I did know that getting Eg seemed to be in a number of people's minds. But a nasty thought started to grow in my head.

There was no time for that now though. What was I to do? Well it was quite straightforward really. We just had to drive a stake through her heart and cut off her head. But it was no good. I wasn't made for that sort of thing. And think of the mess.

She was talking in a foreign language now. It sounded very threatening. I wondered if she was putting a curse on me.

I had a sudden thought. "Don't let her bite you, Frank," I said. But he was holding her carefully away from his body.
"I don' like this, Eg" he said. "She's reel nasty. Can I get rid of her?"

We dumped her outside, rushed back in and locked the door. I hoped none of the neighbours saw. We'd had some funny looks about Josh. It wouldn't go down well if I'd been seen assaulting an old lady.

She wasn't there for long. A car screeched up and took her off. I wasn't surprised to see who the driver was. I returned to the kitchen and looked at the umbrella. The pointed tip had some stuff smeared on it and I carefully washed it down the sink. As Frank said, she was a real nasty lady. Poisonous in every way.
"She come to see the big man," Frank said. "She not nice at all. She said he'd better take me apart an' start again."
Nasty she might be but not without common sense I thought. Poor old Frank.
"Do you know who she is?" I asked.

"I dunno" said Frank. He seemed a bit upset. "She kept talking about her husband. On an' on. Somefink about his head. She was reel angry."

I felt my heart sink into my boots out of the toes and into the drain. Oggy. A husband. A head. Oh help! The powers of darkness were lining up against us. It was Dad, Mum, Tabitha, Frank and me against Big Drac, Mrs. Arshog and lord knows who else. I felt sick.

Frank had started to cry. "I dun my arm again, Eg. I fink it's goin' to fall off."

CHAPTER 14

I almost longed for the time when I had the simple problem of getting enough blood for Josh and the Scurfs. I had two problems now. The first was how to stop Frank falling apart. The second was how to escape assassination by Mrs. A and Big Drac.

Frank was in a panic. First he'd clutch his left arm. Then he'd wail about the big man and the nasty lady knowing where we were. I was relieved when Tabitha turned up. She gave Frank a cuddle and he quietened down a bit.
"You can have a prize if you're really good until lunch" she said.
Frank brightened up. "What's the prize?" he asked.
We settled on a tin of dog food.
I felt a bit envious of Frank. There's a lot to be said for being easily satisfied. I mean it's not a bad deal is it being able to lose your worries in a plate full of Pedigree Chum.
Unfortunately it didn't work for Tabitha and me. But there were compensations. Tabitha was a great support and had all sorts of helpful ideas.
"We'd better go to the Scurf's old house," said I.
"That's the first place they'll look" Tabitha replied.
She was right.
"We'd better ask Mum and Dad."
"It's safer if they don't know where you are. Safer for them too."
She was right about that too.
"We'd better go and stay in a hotel."

"You've got no money and Frank would stick out."
Yes, I didn't fancy breakfast at a hotel with Frank.
I'm afraid my friend's been hurt in an accident and
he thinks he's a dog. Could we have a bowl of milk
and a plate of dog food please."

You don't have to be a genius to work out what we
did in the end. We rang his lordship. I got Boris
first.
"Is everything all right, Mr. Egbert?" he asked.
"No it is not." I felt a bit angry. After all whose fault
was this. The vampire's den hadn't been my idea.
"We've had Mrs. Arshog call with a poisoned
umbrella. There was a silence. I added, "Do you
know Mrs. Arshog?"
"I'll get his lordship," he said.
There was a long wait. I thought about the telephone
bill. It took my mind off things.
His lordship came on. I explained what had
happened. That took a while. Then I waited for his
advice.
He said, "How did she look?"
"I don't understand," I said.
"Agnes, Mrs. Arshog, how did she look? Did she
seem well?"
This wasn't real. I was speechless. Or nearly
speechless. I said, "She had heavy makeup on, so I
wouldn't see she was a vampire. She was old but
terribly strong."
"That's Agnes," he said with satisfaction. "She used
to be my favourite great aunt. You remember. The
one I told you about."
I remembered. The one with a taste for chopping
people's heads off. The one who reminded him of

208

Ma. I couldn't see any similarity between them except for a warlike tendency. But I suppose he was remembering her when she was younger.

His lordship was off down memory lane. "There was a dreadful fuss when she married Arshog. Everyone called her a traitor and none of our family ever spoke to her again. And they thought it disgusting that Arshog was so much younger. He was what you would now call a toy boy."

That figured. Just the sort of toy Mrs. Arshog would choose. My problems were forgotten. Not by me, but by his lordship. He added, "I was sorry it happened. I saw her once again but we didn't speak. I'd be pleased to see her again." That hadn't stopped him from sending Arshog's head back to her, I thought. "That's why I sent the head back," he said. "I thought she'd like to keep it."

This was gross. Then he said, "She's got a bad temper you know. You'll have to be very careful of her, especially if she's with Vladimir. They're a dangerous combination." This was not news to me. I wondered if I should have rung the Samaritans instead.
"I know that," I said. "What I don't know is where to go and what to do."
"I think you'd better stay with us," he said. "At the house we're renting. We'll be over in a day or so or so. Your father's arranging a live concert for us. Has he told you?"

He had. The question was who hadn't he told. The seats were going to sell out as soon as they went on sale. It was the group's first live concert. Until now that had been ruled out by Ma; studio sets and videos only. It seemed Ma had now been over-ruled. They were all going to be sorry about that.

CHAPTER 15

Frank had been very quiet. From time to time he muttered about his arm but I took no notice. But now I saw that he held his arm in an odd way. Almost as if it was going to fall off.
"How's your arm Frank?" I asked.
He sniffed tearfully. "I'ts reel dun in Eg. I dunno wot to do. The big man fix it usual."
Tabitha rolled Frank's shirt sleeve up. His arm had been sewn on above the elbow and it was loose. So was his wrist. Really it was. He was quite right. He was beginning to fall apart.
"How did the big man mend it?" asked Tabitha.
"He got this sort of glue an' he rubbed it on," replied Frank.
My worst dreams about Frank were coming true. He was glued together.
"Don't worry Frank," I said. "I'll fix it for you."

We kept him happy with a tin of dog food and put him to bed early. What were we going to do, I wondered. Superglue perhaps. Tabitha said, "That horrid Drac man must have the stuff for Frank in his house. We'll have to burgle it." I didn't like the idea but she was right. It was either that or watch Frank get smaller bit by bit.

Mum and Dad were away for the next night, so we did it then. We hid in big Drac's garden. It was nerve wracking, especially when Frank kept snuffling. But at about one a.m. Big Drac and Mrs. Arshog came out and drove off.

We had to break a window to get in. Big Drac owed me one of those I thought as I overcame my law-abiding instincts. Inside, Frank knew the way. He led us through narrow corridors to Big Drac's laboratory.

I wasn't very impressed by this. It was dirty and there were a good few empty bottles of whisky on the floor. But Frank knew where to find what he wanted. It was in a big plastic bottle. A newspaper was lying open on the bench beside it and I wrapped it up in that. As we went out I saw a big notebook on top of a filing cabinet. That looks important, I thought, and put it under my arm.

CHAPTER 16

We got home at dawn. Frank rubbed the gunge from the bottle all over his arm. He was a lot happier. Getting himself together, as you might say.

We put Frank to bed. Then Tabitha crashed out. I was tired but I made the mistake of looking at the notebook I'd taken, and I couldn't put it down.

The notebook was a sort of diary and I can't do better than set out the bits that suddenly made me so awake.

"I'll get even" it said. "I'm not having my own father treat me like that. And I'll fix that horrid spotty boy who caused all the trouble."

I got up and looked in the mirror. Not a spot. I'll write to him I thought. How dare he. But maybe there was something else I should put in the letter. I read on.

There was a lot of rambling stuff and then, "Years of work," it said. "I've done it. A break through. Life. I can make Life. I know it. I'm sending all the details to the Medical Association." Big Drac had discovered how to make a monster and wanted to share his secret with his fellow doctors.

The next three weeks of the diary were all about how famous he'd be and so on. Then, "The swine have sent my papers back. They say they only do non fiction. I'll get them." This page of the diary was stained and had a ring on it from the bottom of a bottle. I found the rest of the writing impossible to read. But it was clear that a lot of people were going to be got.

I read on. The birth of Frank hadn't been simple. "Where do I find a body?" Big Drac wrote. "All those morons out there and I can't find one measly body. They'll be sorry. You just wait till I'm famous." Later he wrote, "Perhaps I should start on dogs and cats first." Then he wrote, "It's not perfect but it'll have to do. I can only get a body in bits, an arm here, a leg there and so on. But it's a start."

A few weeks later he wrote, "Heaven help us, it's going to be ugly. But I've got hold of a good brain. It won't be stupid." Something had gone badly wrong hadn't it.

Frank was brought to life a month later. "I've done it," wrote the proud father. "I've created Life. He'll show the world what I can do." A week later he wasn't so sure, and Frank had been christened. "Thing is hopeless," Big Drac wrote. "I think the brain must have gone off. I put it in the fridge and I should have kept it in the deep freeze. It's just like a baby. No memories left. I've even had to teach it how to eat." He hadn't done a very good job.

There were weeks of complaints about poor old Frank. One particularly caught my eye. "I tried not giving Thing the anti-rejection ointment and his arm started to fall off after a week. It's not much use if I can only keep it going with that expensive stuff." Big

Drac not only wanted the best, he wanted it as cheap as possible.

Later: "I met that horrid boy and his revolting girlfriend in the supermarket. They attacked me." I knew Big Drac's hold on reality wasn't very strong but this was ridiculous. A little later: "At last I've found a use for Thing. It's strong and stupid and I'm going to send it after that Egbert boy. Thing can chop his head off. Then I'll stop giving Thing the ointment and it can fall to bits and I'll start again." Poor old Frank. He'd certainly had a deprived childhood.

The next bit confirmed my fears. "Who should turn up on my doorstep but Great Aunt Agnes! What a pleasure to meet a member of the family with standards." Great Aunt Agnes and Big Drac had found a common interest in hatred of his lordship, the Scurfs and Eg. And the nearest and most available was guess who. It was not news to me but it was still depressing.

Agnes sounded as nutty as Big Drac. "She's quite demented about Arshog," he wrote. "She's had his head preserved and carries it round in a bag. When she's at home she keeps it on the mantlepiece. But she's a powerful ally. Together we'll fix them."

That was just before he sent Frank after me. Next was a lot of abuse about me stealing Frank. But then he wrote, "Agnes says not to worry and that Thing was best put in the dustbin. Anyway that's where he'll end up in a week or two without the ointment and good riddance." I'd better not let Frank see this I thought, before I remembered he couldn't read.

The next entry was made after Mrs. Arshog's visit to me. "Agnes tried to bite that nasty little squirt but Thing got in the way. He won't last much longer. Anyway I told Agnes we will wait for the rest of them. I know they're coming to this country soon. Then we'll finish them off."

Then he wrote, "We need help. None of the family here will even talk to us. Well, we'll have to help ourselves, won't we".

That was the end. What did he mean I wondered. I put the diary away. Then I cleaned up Frank's bottle of ointment and put it in the fridge. I picked up the newspaper I'd wrapped it in, glanced at it, and threw it in the bin.

It took a minute or so for the words on the page to get through to my tired brain. Then I got the paper out of the bin. "Mystery virus strikes town," it said.

You won't be surprised at the symptoms. Coma, unconsciousness, apparent death and then a sudden recovery. Yes, Big Drac and Mrs. Arshog had been helping themselves. Somewhere out there was a bunch of newly created vampires; angry, hungry and ready to do what they were told in exchange for plenty of the red stuff.

CHAPTER 17

We met Grandpa and the Vampires, as they arrived discreetly in their specially chartered jet. I introduced his lordship to Frank.

"Hello mister," said Frank. His lordship took Frank's hand very gently as if it might fall off. Very wise. "How nice to meet you dear fellow," he said. "We freaks of nature must stick together."

Very true. If Frank didn't stick together he'd fall apart.

Frank was very impressed by his lordship. "That old man's reel polite" he said. He thought a bit. "What's a freak, Eg?" he said.

There are some things it's better not to know.

"That old man's the big man's Dad," I said.

Frank's eyes bulged. I thought they were going to pop out. He walked quickly back to the coach sucking his thumb.

Dad had arranged a coach. It was a bit of a come down from the usual Mercedes, but more practical. We had security guards driving in front and behind, all the way to the big country house the group had rented.

We had a party when we got to there. It was really good to see them all. It was clear that Bag and Katherine, his new woman, were very close, and I couldn't resist a sideways glance at her. She knew what was in my mind and came searching for me later. "'E is so young, but so mature," she said. She was certainly half right. She clutched my arm. "I can give 'im what 'e needs," she said. "What is age? Ve are as young as ve feel."

I felt one hundred years old. She hadn't told him had she. And the others had all copped out. There was only one thing to do. I copped out too. "He's a wonderful human being," I said. "You are very lucky."

Then she said, "You 'ave seen Agnes, my elderly relative. 'Ow is she?" What had Agnes got that I hadn't got I thought. Perhaps I should join the Salvation Army.

"She looked pale but well," I said.

"I am so pleased," she replied. More than I was.

I found myself next to Josh. Sandra was saying to Mum, "Yea, sociology an' psychology go well togever. Don't they Josh," and she shook his arm. "An' religious studies is really interesting. Ain't it Josh," another shake. I thought Mum and Dad would like this, but I could see they didn't really.

But Dad was really mellow. "Sold out already," he said to Ma. "The whole concert has gone".

"No mirrors I 'ope" said Ma.

"Nothing that can't be covered up," said Dad.

Oh for a time machine: don't do it Dad.

"I'll 'ave an inspection," said Ma.

Much good that did. But all these worries were yet to come and we didn't worry, we had a good time.

That night we had a council of war. His lordship said, "We don't have to look for them, they will come here to us." That wasn't news to me, it was just saying what the problem was. "They'll come at night in the early hours," he said.

He was so wrong.

That night I looked at Frank's ointment. At this rate it would last no more than another week.

CHAPTER 18

They were up all night chatting, which wasn't surprising. I gave up in the early hours and went to bed.

I was woken by Frank. He'd brought me breakfast and had he made a dreadful mess of it! I looked at the tray. As well as the slops on it, there was a big bowl of milk, and a piece of toast topped with a slice of dog food. Frank was hopping from one foot to the other.

"An' and I opened the tin myself," he said. "Do you like it Eg? I got it special for you."

I didn't know what to say. Then I said, "That looks really good Frank." He smiled and looked expectant, and waited.

Well, dog food doesn't taste so bad really, but then we only bought the best for Frank.

Mum and Dad had stayed over, and I found them downstairs with Tabitha at the breakfast table. They tried not to laugh when I came in. Dad kept making woof woof noises, but I ignored him. I thought he was very childish.

Dad had a busy day ahead. The next day the group were to be interviewed on TV. Not in a studio, but here in the house.

His lordship got up mid afternoon. "How can we defend ourselves?" I asked him. "We need help."

Instead of giving me a lecture on how sporting it was to be outnumbered his lordship said, "Yes. I've spoken to Igor and he'll bring help."

Igor, with his black beard and broad shoulders, turned up at dusk. With him were six sinister-looking vampires. I was glad they were on our side. They kept watch all night, two of them at the main gate. But there was no attack.

The next day started badly. It began with a phone call from Tabitha's father. I only heard bits.
"Out of control ... groupie ... taking in hand ..."
I got the general picture.
Tabitha put the phone down and said, "They say they're coming to take me back. I promised to be home by yesterday." Now she told me! I didn't know which I fancied facing least, Tabitha's Dad or Big Drac's vampire hoards.

I thought I'd have a chat with Josh. Because of the TV interview he'd got up when he'd normally be in bed. He was shaving. Not that Josh needed to shave every day, which was just as well. Being a vampire has its advantages but it makes it difficult to look after your appearance. I mean you can't see yourself in mirrors. So Josh had to shave by feel. His lordship had bought a job lot of digital cameras, and when they wanted to see how they looked they'd get a quick photo taken. Ma said it was conceited to keep looking in mirrors anyway. But Josh wasn't really interested in my problems. All he'd say about Tabitha's parents was, "Rather you than me. And you'd better keep them away from Dad."

Tabitha's father was always angry. He did have the virtue of consistency. Good things, bad things, funny things, sad things: he'd be angry about all of them.

Tabitha's mother was very mild. She didn't have much chance to be anything else. She was always holding Tabitha's Dad back or apologising for him. And he and Dad didn't get on. Dad didn't mind freaking out himself once in a while but he didn't like other people doing it.

Frank was my other worry. But I could see I wasn't going to get much help from Josh. I called on his lordship. He shook his head. "The only person I knew with an interest in this sort of thing was a Mary Shelley," he said. "Charming woman, unreliable husband. Both long since dead I'm afraid. No, only Vladimir can help."

What a relief! Everything was solved. All I had to do was ask Big Drac to sort it out. I could see what sort of help I'd get there. A large black bin liner to put the bits in.

I checked up on Frank. He was with Freddie. It was no surprise that Freddie was not to be interviewed. What was surprising was how he and Frank got on. They'd adopted one another. And Freddie had told Frank that he was a monster too.

"I'm so lucky," said Frank. "I got reel friends now." He wiped his nose on his sleeve. "They did a reel good job on Freddie didn't they. You can't see the joins." He sighed and added, "Perhaps the man what done Freddie could take me apart and put me back together proper."

Poor old Frank. If I didn't come up with something soon he'd be being put back together by the big surgeon in the sky. I wondered if Frank could go to heaven or whether the place was already taken by the original owners of his body. Excuse me sonny, but that's my seat, get the hell out of here. That would just be poor Frank's luck.

CHAPTER 19

The TV people arrived at 11 a.m. There was the interviewer, who I recognised, the director, a camera man and the lighting man.

Dad let them in and they were all really creepy to one another. The interviewer's name was Bob. "How lovely to meet you face to face," he said to Dad. "This is Dick," he added, pointing to the director, "and Fred and Simon," pointing at the others. It wasn't going to be hard to remember Dick's name I thought as he got through a day's supply of supers, lovelies and terrifics in about five minutes.

And Dad, my dear old Dad? I'm sorry to say he was as bad as the rest of them. But that's show business folks. I could see he didn't mean a word of it though. And nor did they.

The interview was to be held in a big sitting room on the first floor, overlooking the grounds. Dad had asked me to sit in on it.
"You can be message boy," he said. As he led the way up the stairs I realised I hadn't mentioned Tabitha's parents to him.

His lordship sat in his studded leathers. Ma sat beside him on a long settee. She wore a black silk dress with a slit up the side and the biggest diamond necklace I have ever seen: something his lordship pillaged centuries before I expect. She offered her hand to Bob as if she expected him to kiss it.

"It iz ver' good of you to visit our leetle 'ome," she said.

I sat with Dad by the window as the interview progressed.

"Freddie? No, Freddie 'e iz not well, he iz in ze bed under ze doctor."

"Charlie? Charlie 'e writes a fabulous new number. 'E work on it night and day, an' 'e iz exhausted."

Bob started on his lordship. "Grandpa, if I may call you that?"

His lordship gave Bob a look he usually reserved for shop keepers who'd tried to charge him too much.

Bob continued undeterred. "Don't you think your vampire image goes over the top sometimes?"

As I looked through the window I saw a familiar car coming down the long drive.

"We may have a few surprises for you," replied his lordship.

My Mum has a saying, "Don't tempt providence." It's good advice.

I had a word with Dad and tiptoed out. When the doorbell rang I was there first.

Tabitha's surname was Edwards, and Mr. and Mrs. Edwards were standing on the doorstep.

"Hah," said Mr Edwards. "We've come to take our daughter home."

I led them to the kitchen and Mum and Tabitha.

"How nice to see you," said Mrs. Edwards to Mum.

"A disgrace," said Mr. Edwards. "It's a disgrace." He pointed to me. "He's a disgrace." He spoke to Tabitha. "You're a disgrace".

Nobody spoke. There wasn't much you could do with him when he'd got to this point.

225

"I want to see your father young man," he shouted.

Back I crept in to the interview. Sandra was droning on about Josh's exams. Poor Bob kept trying to interrupt her but without success. From time to time Sandra let her blouse fall off one shoulder.

I whispered to Dad. We had to shut Mr. Edwards up and get rid of him. Dad didn't want to come but he knew he had to. As he was pretending to make his mind up, I looked at the figures running out of the woods.

Bob had managed to shut Sandra up and Bag was talking now. As I listened to him a nasty thought started to trickle into my mind and then down my spine. I did a double take back to the window. No, it wasn't a dream, nor an optical illusion. They were coming in all directions, across the park. We were under attack.

I nudged Dad and pointed. His lips moved in a silent favourite expression. He'll say, this is all we need, I thought. He muttered, "This is all we need. I'll hold the fort here. Go and wake Igor and the others up at once."

I rushed downstairs. First things first. I dashed into Igor's room and shook him awake and said that we were under attack. Then I bolted the front door. I dashed into the kitchen to do the back door. I'd completely forgotten about Tabitha's parents.
"About time too," humphed Mr. Edwards. He seemed a bit calmer. Then, "Where's your father?"
"Er, he'll be along in a minute," I said. "He's in the television interview."
"I've explained all about that," said Mum. "Isn't it wonderful." Good old Mum, I could see she'd been trying to get round Mr. Edwards.
"I've asked Tabitha's parents to stay on for a drink so they can meet Bob after the interview," added Mum.
Drinks at the funeral feast perhaps.

But there was no time to waste. We didn't want the vampire hoard bursting into the kitchen and spoiling Mr. Edwards' cup of tea. I went to the back door and bolted it.
"What on earth are you doing that for?" said Tabitha.
"Er, the burglar alarm test," I said. "You know, all the doors and shutters have to be closed and locked for it. Igor insists." I looked at her and Mum very hard.

"We've got to have it tested before our other visitors arrive, his lordship's son and his friends. They're on the way right now."

The penny dropped. "I'd forgotten all about it," said Mum. "Now you and Tabitha run off and see to the shutters." As we closed the last set of shutters I saw the first of the enemy run onto the terrace. Big Drac had chosen well, they were all fit and young and they were armed with clubs. I could hear hammering on the front door.

"Your father will go bananas," I said to Tabitha. "You get back to the kitchen and shut him up. Think of something. I must go upstairs."

As I entered the interview room Dad was holding forth. "It's the fans, the fans," he declaimed, waving his hands in the air. "They love the group, but they cause such a lot of trouble. Well, that's the price of fame. Ha, ha." He looked thoughtfully out of the window. On the terrace a group of young men and women were pounding away at the door and shutters. A few stragglers still walked across the park. Behind them an unfit Big Drac struggled with what looked like a bundle of axes under his arm.

His lordship spoke. "If you will excuse me I had better leave you for a moment. Perhaps I can restore some order."
Ma rose. "'An' I must go too. Vere my 'usband go I go too. Ve are inseparable."
Dad said, "I'd better go as well."

His lordship added. "I think Bag should come as well, he's a great favourite with the fans."

But Bob wasn't going to be separated from a good story so easily. "I'll come with you," he said and followed us, closing the door behind him.

"I think 'is lordship will deal viz ze fans better on 'is own," said Ma.

But Bob would have none of that. "No, no" he replied. "It'll be a wonderful addition to the interview. We mustn't miss a thing."

Ma stuck her fist under his nose. "'Ere," she said. "Jew see this? Well, if yer don't want a bunch of fives up yer conk, just get back in that room and shut yer gob."

That shut Bob up all right. He blinked as if he couldn't believe what he'd heard.

Then Ma said, "I must inseest 'is lordship's wishes are respected."

Bob just stared. Then he turned slowly and went back into the room, shaking his head. Ma locked the door behind him.

CHAPTER 21

In the hallway we found Igor, Mum and Tabitha. Igor reported to his lordship. "I need one person for each room downstairs and one for each door. That way we will know when they break through. They will. You can't defend the ground floor. We'll have to hold them back eventually on the main stairs."

"But they 'ave only clubs," said Katherine. "Ve go out and chop some of zer 'eads off. Zey are not warriors. Zey vill run avay."

Good breeding always shows in the end I thought. Katherine was a chip off the old block.

His lordship shook his head. "Not in this country" he said. "And we have witnesses here."

From the noise it sounded as if they'd started on the front door with an axe. Charlie and Bag pushed heavy furniture in front of it. I suddenly realised that Tabitha and Mum were here but no Mr. and Mrs. Edwards.

"Where are your parents?" I asked Tabitha.

"I've locked them in one of the cellars," she said. "I told them terrorists must be trying to kidnap the group. Dad took one look through the back-door keyhole and went down the cellar like a lamb."

"Where's the key," I asked. "In the lock," she replied.

That was no good. Once they were through the front door they'd find the cellar and it would be lamb chops. Why should I worry? But he was Tabitha's Dad, and Mrs. Edwards was very nice.

"I'll fix it," I said and went down to the cellars. I could see the light was on in one and I turned the key. They must have felt really bad! I'd never seen

Mr. Edwards pleased to see me before. I gave him the key.

"Lock yourselves in and turn off the light and don't make a sound," I said. There was a dreadful crash of glass upstairs. They must have got through the shutters.

Bang went the cellar door, the key turned, and the light went off. It was time to go. But I noticed the next-door cellar and something in it caught my eye. I put the light on. I was right. I had an idea. I and the idea ran upstairs to his lordship.

"Where would we be without you dear boy?" he said. "Put your mother and Tabitha onto it." I did that and returned.

His lordship was now talking to Igor. "We are outnumbered. Have the sabres laid out upstairs just in case. There was a crash as the front door fell down. Igor's men manned the barricade of furniture behind it. The other doors leading from the hall were also blocked with furniture.

Katherine was waving a huge kitchen knife. His lordship called to Boris. "Take that thing from Katherine. Find her a club or something that won't draw blood." He smiled, then noted me at his side. "She's a dear girl. She just gets a bit carried away," he said. He added, "I think we're going to need Josh and Sandra. Could you ask them to come down, please".

Bag came up to Katherine. "'Ere darlin' don't yer fink yer'd better take it easy?"

231

"Ach," she shouted. "Ve take these leetle boys an' girls an' chop them in leetle bits and send them back to zeir peasant parents, yes?"

It didn't take her long to see this didn't fit in with the teenage girl-friend bit.

"Ach, my big Bagsey, you protect me, yes?" she said, and gave him a hug.

Boris had arrived with the club. With some difficulty Katherine refused it and gave him the knife, simpering at Bag. Well, you're bound to pick up a few tricks in one hundred and thirty years, aren't you.

I realised I wasn't doing my duty and rushed off upstairs to the interview room. This was full of icy silence. Josh and Sandra looked anxious. Bob was staring gloomily out of the window. Dick and the others were playing cards.

Bob turned as I entered. "Ah," he said. "We came to interview the organ grinders and here we have the monkey instead." Very polite. "I suppose you think we're filming all that rabble outside," continued Bob. "Well you'll be disappointed. We didn't come here for cheap publicity stunts".

Dick interrupted. "Not cheap Bobsey, cost a bundle to set this lot up. Terrific extras, where d'you get them?"

"It's just the fans. They're out of control," I said. I indicated to Josh and Sandra to get out and they

232

slipped through the door. I was about to follow when my jaw dropped.

Through the window I could see a hot air balloon. It had almost sunk to the ground and was trying to regain height. Peering over the basket were a number of heads but I only saw one of them. It was white-haired. I couldn't see the rest of her but I didn't think she'd be wearing her Salvation Army uniform.

"Look at this," said Bob, pointing at the balloon. "Is it really necessary? I mean we came here for a serious interview. Who do you lot think you are?" It was pretty clear who he thought he was.

There was a loud bang downstairs. "I've had enough of this," said Bob and pushed past me through the door. I thought I'd at least keep the other three in, and locked the door behind us.

When I turned round it was as if the scene were frozen. We were on a wide landing. On one side was the door to the interview room. On the other side was a door leading to the rest of the upper house. I could see Tabitha through it.

At the top of the wide stairway stood Boris, Katherine and Ma, then Bag and Charlie and Josh. At the bottom stood Igor's men, Levin, Igor and, right in front, his lordship.

In front of them lay a pile of very expensive antique firewood. In front of the firewood was a crowd of ugly

233

looking vampires. They hadn't learned to control their teeth yet and some of them were hanging out like walrus tusks.

Behind this lot was Big Drac. He had a drinking flask in one hand and a megaphone in the other. There was a moment of silence. The barricades were down. It was high noon, the big shoot out.

CHAPTER 22

"How nice to see you all" said Bob.

All eyes switched Bobwards. "I suppose you're all hoping to get on the 9 O'Clock News," he sneered. "Well dream on. I wouldn't hire you lot for a toilet commercial."

Friend and foe looked fascinated at this unexpected interlude. Bob descended the stairs pushing through the defenders until he stood by his lordship. "And as for you, Grandpa, or his lordship or whatever you call yourself." Bob broke off. He'd noticed the teeth. "Now," he said. "That's good, that's really good. Very clever. Quite convincing."
One of the enemy sucked his teeth and then pushed them out again.
"Amazing," said Bob. "Who's your special effects man? I take it all back. I'll get the boys down and we'll do some filming."

He walked towards the dumbstruck audience on the other side and clasped a young man by the shoulders. "Open your mouth so I can get a good look." He took one of the teeth in his fingers and tugged it. "Say, how do you fix these things on?"

But Bob was not to find out, at least not the easy way. Big Drac had kept his troops starved of blood. Not so much as to make them feel ill, but enough to

235

make them bad tempered and in a hurry for the extra ration he promised them once the victory was won.

The temptation was too great for Bob's new friend. He cut short the dental examination by burying his jaw in Bob's neck. There was a lot of slurping.

His lordship shouted. "Hold them back Vladimir, and get that boy off him. The man is a well-known journalist. If he dies you'll be ruined as well as us."

Big Drac was silent for a few more slurps. Then he called, "Pull him off, and let them take their friend back where he belongs." Then he cackled and hiccupped. "He can live as a slave of the family now."

It was just as well Big Drac was a bit drunk. Otherwise he would have worked out that one more body on top of a pop group and its relations wouldn't make much difference.

Bob was carried upstairs and into the interview room. "He fainted," I said. "He'll be fit in a minute or so." Lucky old Bob was going to live to a ripe old age.

CHAPTER 23

As I locked the door of the interview room yet again I remembered the balloon. I rushed and told Igor. "They must plan to get on the roof and attack us from the rear," he said. He called two of his men and sent them with Bag and Charlie to the roof. "They'll rush us soon," said Igor. "We'll hold them off for a while but the numbers are wrong. If we weren't in such a law-abiding country we could cut them down in no time. Never mind. We'll hold them here for a bit." He patted me on the shoulder. "Then we'll see how good your plan is."

Yes, I had a plan. No, it did not involve water pistols. And yes, you will have to wait to see if it worked or not.

There was the sound of more banging and then a commotion at the back of the hall. I heard a familiar angry voice.
"How dare you. Put me down ....   Arghh."
Mr. Edwards had seen the teeth as they dragged him and Mrs Edwards up from outside the cellar they had foolishly left. I watched their progress to Big Drac. He shouted for silence. I heard Mr. Edwards say, "Haven't I seen you somewhere before?"
" Aha," said Big Drac triumphantly. "I know who you are. You're the parents of that horrid boy's girlfriend. Well you just stay here and drink it all in and enjoy yourselves. Because after we've fixed this lot we'll be drinking you in, every little drop in your dear little veins."

Mrs. Edwards went out like a light. Mr. Edwards said "Er, haven't I see you at Rotary? Then he tried to shake Big Drac's hand. Then he crossed himself. Then he said, "All right, the joke's over now." Then he didn't say anything because someone hit him over the head with a club.

I made my way to the roof. From the main landing I went to a stairway. This led to a long attic. Our defences, the great plan, were laid out here. I hoped they worked. From the room a ladder led to the roof.

Up there I saw Mum, Dad, Tabitha, Sandra and Katherine and the others. I also saw the balloon. This kept going up and down slowly like a yo-yo as they tried to land it on the long flat roof. Afterwards I learnt that Mrs. A. had hired the balloon for a childrens' party and overpowered the driver. It was clear that Mrs. A. had not been to ballooning classes.

There were greasy looking splash marks on the roof. "Look out!" shouted Tabitha as the balloon passed over. Something splashed by me and I felt a sting on my hand. Mrs. A. was bombarding us with boiling oil. As my Dad says, it's difficult to get a leopard to change its spots. "She's getting better," said Tabitha. "She'll manage to land soon."

Before that happened Ma arrived Josh and Dad followed. "The others are coming," he said, and they did, Boris with the sabres under his arm. Then his lordship, Boris, Levin and Igor stood at the top of the stairway, clubs at the ready.

"And now my young friend," said his lordship to me, "We will see if your plan works."

CHAPTER 24

We could hear the shouting getting nearer until it reached the room below. A few heads poked up above the stairway and got whacked. But no more heads appeared after that, and a strange silence fell on the room below.

We sat and waited. I could hear someone shouting. It sounded like Big Drac. Then the laughter started, quietly at first and then louder and louder.

The balloon passed by a few feet above our heads. We ducked, but Mrs. A. had evidently run out of oil. She screeched in some foreign tongue. "Good day Aunt Agnes," called his lordship, but she shook her fist at him. "I think we'd better see what's going on below," he said.

The long attic room was full of vampires. Some lay flat out. A few were dancing and laughing. But most were sitting on the floor with silly grins on their faces, giggling.

On the table at the end of the room lay the remains of his lordship's cellar, carried up here by Mum and Tabitha. Bottles and bottles of the red stuff, and all opened and ready for Big Drac's crew. Blood-thirsty wasn't in it. They'd drunk themselves silly.

Big Drac was rushing round the room, shaking one, slapping the face of another. As we climbed down he looked up snarling and kicked a couple of giggling bodies.

I'd never seen his lordship look so fierce. You can play with your new friends here Vladimir," he said. "We have other business upstairs. Then I'll decide what to do with you."

Back on the roof, the balloon was sailing down towards us again. But this time one of the occupants had climbed from the basket and was hanging from a rope. As he swept past Igor caught his ankle and Bag leapt and caught the rope. A number of people leapt and caught Bag, who was in danger of sailing off into the sky. The bloke from the balloon lay back gasping.
"Who's the boss here?"
His lordship bowed.
"I surrender," said the man. "You can't be worse than that old bat. She's raving mad. She splashed us all with boiling chip fat and we're all air sick. She said she knew how to fly that thing."
"Take him and his friends downstairs for some refreshment," said his lordship to Levin. Off to the party boys. Drink as much as you like.

The others had climbed out of the basket, all except for Mrs. A. She screeched at us. I didn't understand what she was saying.
"Good gracious," said Boris. "That's no way for a lady to speak."
They turned the balloon basket on its side so she had to crawl out and she found herself standing in front of his lordship.

"Good afternoon Aunt Agnes," he said. "I'm so pleased to see you after all this time. So kind of you to drop in."

After more screeching his lordship replied, "Well, I'm sorry too Aunt Agnes. But Arshog did attack us and he had a fair fight."

Mrs. A. changed into English. "He was a better man than you. Look at you in those ridiculous clothes."

"Perhaps I should have worn my Salvation Army uniform," said his lordship.

That made her cackle. Mind, that sounded more frightening than when she screeched. Then she saw Katherine.

"What's that tart doing here?" she screamed. Bag took Katherine's hand. Mrs. A. cackled, "So that's the poor young man."

I felt like shutting my eyes and putting my fingers in my ears and as I looked round I could see everyone else did too. Mrs. A. was about the spill the best known, best-kept secret in the family.

"You stupid clot of a boy," she said. "Don't you know your little girlfriend is old enough to be your mother's granny?"

There was a gasp as we all breathed in. People studied their toes or the sky. But Bag stuck his chest out, squeezed Katherine's hand and said, "So what? Yer old 'as been. An' I know anyway, an' I don't mind." He kissed Katherine's cheek. "I didn't wanta spoil yer secret darlin'." He pointed a finger at Mrs. A. "You ain't the only one in the family wot likes 'em young, 'cept yer look like five 'undred years old yer old 'ag."

That should have shut her up. But I don't know if Mrs. A. had a reply. We were never to find out for we next heard Big Drac's voice.

This did not say, "Please forgive me and let me go and I won't do it again." No. Instead it said, "And now I've got you, you swine, every one of you." This might seem a bit unrealistic under the circumstances but looking at Big Drac I could see one good reason for taking him seriously. That was the machine gun in his hands and pointing at us.

"What a bounder," I heard Boris mutter.

"Vladimir," called his lordship. "Remember your upbringing and put that peasant's weapon down."

But Big Drac knew he was onto a winner and had entirely lost interest in good manners. "My upbringing," he said, "is something I intend to forget altogether, along with you lot. Now put your hands up."

I looked for help.

"I've tied Levin up," said Big Drac. "I'm not going to run out of anything. I've got plenty of time and plenty of rope." He gave a horrid laugh. "And plenty of stakes."

"He's gone mad," said his lordship to Mrs. A. "What on earth have you been doing getting yourself mixed up with him?"

"But I was so upset about Oggie," she replied, "and Vladimir is the only relation who has spoken to me for one hundred and fifty years. You get very lonely and angry you know."

"Well, try and control him," said his lordship.

Aunt Agnes stepped forward.

"Stop or I shoot," shouted Big Drac.

243

"But I'm your friend Vladimir," she replied. "I'm on your side."

"On your own side, you mad old crone," he said. "I don't need you now."

We stood frozen. This was it. He gave a manic laugh. With his left hand he pulled out a bottle from his pocket, undid the top with his teeth, drained the contents and threw the empty over the edge of the roof.

I heard Igor mutter, "Is it loaded?"

Big Drac fired a shot at a chimney pot. The pot flew apart.

"Who's first?" said Big Drac. "Ah," he said as he pointed at me. "The spotty squirt. You started it all. You step out in front."

As I did so Big Drac pointed the gun at me. I stared, fascinated. "Say goodbye, zit face" he said.

CHAPTER 25

What fascinated me lay behind Big Drac. He stood some metres in front of a set of huge chimneys that stood at one end of the roof. Do not think that I was developing a sudden interest in architecture during my last moments. What I stared at was a familiar face peeping between two of the chimneys. It had dark hair and a hook nose.

As Big Drac bade me goodbye the face disappeared. Then from round the corner of the chimney stack burst Frank, hurling himself like a cannonball onto Big Drac. The gun fired a few shots in the air and clattered across the roof. Frank lay flat out with Big Drac under him.

Frank was a hero. Everyone shook his hand. That seemed unwise to me but he enjoyed it.
"'E iz a real warrior," said Katherine, and gave him a big hug. But Aunt Agnes gave her a dreadful look and she put Frank down quickly.
"Thank goodness you was there," said Ma as she helped him up. "Yore for it mate," she added to Big Drac.

Frank told us his tale. "I was lookin' after Freddie," he said. "Freddie and me was frightened so we hid under the table in the attic. An' then people came in and put fings on it and went away. So we looked on it an' it was all bottles of blood. An' then Freddie he drank too much of it and got all silly so I took him up on the roof and hid him behind the chimney." And there indeed was Freddie. Dead to the world, snoring, and with a big smile on his face.

We all left the roof. In the attic we untied Levin and left him in charge of Big Drac's band with orders to give another drink to any that looked at all sensible.

Dad was the first to remember Bob and his TV crew. He unlocked the door cautiously and he, his lordship and I went in.

Dad put on a great performance, really wicked. "I'm so sorry," he said. "What a mix up there's been. We've got to the bottom of it now." He beamed reassuringly. "You won't believe it." How was Dad going to get out of this one, I wondered. "We're doing a video for the next release. The theme apparently is warfare between rival groups of vampires." He laughed, "I know it sounds silly but the director got the dates mixed up. They were supposed to come next week and they came today. And the director hadn't even told us the theme, so we didn't guess at first what was happening."

Dad's audience didn't look too impressed. He ploughed on, "Once we got going and the boys got their outfits on we shot some really good film, and the special effects were good, weren't they?" This was addressed to Bob. Bob looked uneasy. He felt the place on his neck and smiled nervously.

Dad continued, "I'm sure the video will be good but I don't think we'll use that director again. What did

246

you say your name was?" he said to Dick. That cheered Dick up no end.

Fred and Simon were more difficult to please. "Another hour and we'd have been on time and a half," grumbled Fred. Dad did his best. "Here are some complimentary tickets for the concert." But it was clear that Grandpa and the Vampires were not Fred and Simons' idea of a good night out.

His lordship took over. "A token of appreciation," he said, handing over the cash. That was more like it, and bought time-and-a-half smiles to their faces.

As we saw them off the premises his lordship put his hand on Bob's shoulder. "You don't look well. I suggest you come and finish the interview when you've fully recovered. Just you. When you've had time to reflect. That's a good word, isn't it?" But his lordship made no actual appointment. That proved to be a mistake.

Next were Tabitha's parents. I'd forgotten them. To be more correct I did not wish to remember them. But Tabitha, like a good daughter, had gone to look for them first. She and Mum untied them and sat them in the kitchen, gave her mother a cup of tea and her father a large whisky. I stuck my head round the door. Mr. Edwards had his back to me. I could hear him murmuring. "Outrage ... disgrace .... sue ..... newspapers ..." He was not going to be easy to deal with.

247

After a short council of war his lordship changed out of his leathers into his poshest, most old fashioned and respectable suit. Then he and Dad went in and did a job on Mr. Edwards. "How unforgivable," said his lordship. "Please accept my apologies. A dreadful mixup. We had commissioned a video film for our next release. Vampire battle it was to be called. The fool of a director didn't give us the details and got the dates mixed up and then all those dreadful actors dressed up as vampires arrived. And of course the more we resisted the more they thought we were just acting."

This was going down like what my Dad calls a lead balloon. But his lordship wasn't stupid. "My dear chap," he said to Mr. Edwards. "I have, of course, sacked the director and I do not propose to pay him for today. However, I have spoken to him and he agrees you should be compensated for this terrible experience and he has suggested that I pay the money instead to you." His lordship handed a cheque to Mr. Edwards who looked at it with bulging eyes.

"Goodness me," he said. "I didn't imagine film directors were paid so much." Then he coughed a bit, "Er, well er, I think that's fair compensation for this fellow to pay, don't you, my dear?"

But his lordship hadn't finished. "I'm so pleased we have met, even if I regret the circumstances. We are so very fond of your daughter, she is so beautifully brought up. And such a good companion for Egbert here. Egbert is doing so well in his studies, is he not?" There was a lot more of this sort of thing. So

248

Tabitha stayed on and Mr. and Mrs. Edwards hurried off home to spend the loot.

CHAPTER 26

Big Drac had been tied up and led to the cellar. As they put the rope on he spoke to Frank. "Much good may this do you. That ointment can't last more than another week. Then they'll need more than a needle and cotton to put you back together." And he gave a horrid, bad-breath laugh. Frank whimpered and I tried to comfort him but couldn't think of anything to say.

The trial of Big Drac could not be avoided. I could see how upset his lordship was. "He is still my son," he said. "I cannot be a part of it."
Boris, Igor and Dad were to be the judges. "Who's going to defend him," I asked.
"Defence, Mr. Egbert?" said Boris. "What do we need a defence for?"
"We all know what he's done," added Igor.
"But he's got to have someone to defend him," I said.
Katherine interrupted, "You mean ve hav ze duel to ze death ?"
"No," I replied. "I mean someone speaks for him, puts his point of view, his arguments."
"Huh," said Katherine. " Zat iz for peasants and shop keepers."
Dad said, "Well, he's right really. At any rate, in this country and, er, nowadays."
His lordship spoke. "My dear boy, it was your idea that saved the day. Perhaps we should not pick and choose so among your ideas." He smiled gently, "But who is to speak for Vladimir?"

There was a silence. I could see what was coming. Eg walks into it again. He added, "Well, dear boy, you are appointed to the defence."

The trial was held in the interview room. We waited for Levin to bring Big Drac up.

"What he did is unforgivable," said Boris.

"No civilized society can put up with that sort of thing," agreed Igor.

"How can he have done it?" added Boris.

"Yes," said Igor. "He has become totally depraved."

I could see Dad was feeling he should say something. "It is a dreadful thing for a son to try to kill his father," he contributed.

Boris and Igor both looked at him in a puzzled way.

"Oh that," said Boris. "Yes, to be sure, that's very bad too, although these things happen from time to time."

"Then what are you talking about" asked Dad.

"The machine gun of course," said Boris. "Such shame on the family. We'll never live it down."

Igor shook his head sadly. "How can he have done such a terrible thing?" he said.

Big Drac was led in, his hands bound behind his back and stood before the judges. Everyone else including Frank sat behind Big Drac. I stood beside him.

"What are you standing there for you ugly squirt?" he said to me.

"I'm, er, defending you," I said hesitantly.

"Huh," he said. "They might as well have given me Thing. Defence! Put me in a room with you and a battle axe and I'd show you defence. I'd turn that spotty head of yours into a football."

251

"Order, order," Boris raised his voice. Then he read out Big Drac's name in full. That took a while. "You are accused of taking up a machine gun to achieve your purposes, of treason, of treachery and of conduct unbecoming to a gentleman and vampire."

Igor whispered in his ear. "Oh yes," said Boris, "and of attempting to kill your father and lots of other people." He added, "including me."

"Get lost," said Big Drac.

"Guilty," said Boris. "Now what have you got to say for yourself?"

"I don't answer to my father's servants," said Big Drac. "You get back to the butler's pantry where you belong."

Boris went red. "At least I know how to behave like a gentleman," he said.

Igor intervened. "Egbert, you're the defender. Do some defending."

"Well he did all these things," I said. "But it wasn't completely his fault." This was really difficult, but as I thought I got more into it. "He had a deprived childhood," I added. "His mother died when he was a baby, and his father wasn't able to give him the affection he needed. He always wanted his father to be proud of him but he could never succeed. Then he saw the Scurfs break all the rules and his father let them get away with it. So he went mad and broke all the rules himself."

There was a long and uneasy silence after that. Big Drac stood like stone. I heard an unaccustomed series of sniffs from his lordship behind me.

Igor sighed heavily. "There may be much truth in what you say young advocate, but those were

252

difficult days as those who were there know. Anyway, because we are dealt a bad hand we are not entitled to refuse to play. We have to deal with whatever we are given. What do you say to that?"

"He was all alone," I said.

"He lived by the sword, why should he not perish by it?" said Igor. I looked at the stake and hammer in the corner.

Igor added, "How else are the innocent to be protected from him?"

I was at a loss. "Have you any ideas?" I whispered to Big Drac. He said, "Next time I'll get a lawyer with a good primary school education, smart arse."

It was then I that had the idea. "Can I have a word in private with him," I asked. When I put it to Big Drac he didn't like it. In fact, at one point, I thought he would refuse and take it on the chin, or rather in the chest. But in the end he had to agree.

Back before the Court I said, "We have a proposal, a deal to put to you. In exchange for his life he will promise to be good in future." I waited for the hoots behind me to die down, and added, "and then he will disclose the secret formula for Frank's ointment." I could see they didn't like it. Well, Big Drac was dangerous and would be up to no good again, that was for sure.

Frank got up and shuffled to the front. "Pleese, pleese everyone, I dun want to fall to bits, especial when I got all you new friends. An' I'll be good and not spill my milk, an' I'll look after Freddie reel good."

Igor, Boris and Dad put their heads together. Then Igor said, "This involves everyone and we must look to his lordship for guidance."

His lordship stood up. "What can I say?" he said. "My son is condemned. Should I release him to strike again? But should we put him away, to condemn Frank to death? We all owe our lives to Frank and, truly, in him the whole is greater than the sum of the parts."

I couldn't have put it better myself. "What's he mean?" whispered Frank to me anxiously. "Why is he talking about parts?"

"Don't worry Frank," I said, "you're going to get the ointment."

Frank was so pleased he thanked everyone, even Big Drac.

"I hope it sticks your stupid mouth together," said Big Drac to him.

CHAPTER 27

Big Drac was sent on his way. He'd hired a bus to bring his troops. His lordship paid the driver off and told him to go home. Igor and I then escorted Big Drac to the gates.

"You can walk home," said Igor. "And I know where you live. One more trick from you and that's it, right through your heart, if we can find it. You'll get no more chances."

Big Drac looked dreadful. His face was grey and he kept dribbling. His clothes were torn and dirty. He spat at Igor, made a rude sign at us and hobbled down the road. I only wish I could say that I never saw him again.

There remained the small problem of Big Drac's new followers. We couldn't exactly send them home. I must say it worried me who'd look after them. Where would they get the blood they needed? How would they be taught how to be well-behaved vampires?

His lordship was most relaxed when I tried to discuss it with him. "Don't take the cares of the world on your shoulders, my dear friend" he said. "We'll find somewhere for them."

I didn't know what his lordship had in mind. If he was thinking of taking them home with him he'd have to make other arrangements. The day after the battle we received a message to say a mob of locals had burnt down his lordship's house at night. The fire brigade let it burn to the ground and then put the embers out with holy water.

But his lordship seemed unperturbed. All he said was, "The fire insurance is up to date isn't it Boris?" and later, "I'd grown tired of living there and it was rather hot and sunny for such as us."

Mrs. A., Aunt Agnes, was put in charge of the new members of the family and organised classes for them. She gave lectures on how to avoid mirrors, cooking without garlic and how to bite discreetly if you really had to. There were other classes on the dangers of drinking too much of you know what, and a series of lessons on "Unacceptable Vampire Behaviour, or How to Avoid a Stake Through the Heart." Boris taught the men sabre fighting and Katherine gave lectures on vampire traditions and the family history.

Big Drac and Aunt Agnes had taken care only to choose young single people living on their own. But they had friends and parents, and Mum and Tabitha helped write letters explaining how they were going away for some time and would be out of touch.

Igor and his men went home. Igor shook my hand. "I hope it is not so long before we meet again." This time he was right.

One evening I turned the TV to Bob's usual programme, but there was no Bob. "Bob can't be with us tonight," said his substitute. "But I'm pleased to tell you he has made a miraculous recovery from what we feared was a fatal illness." Welcome to the club Bob. Better buy yourself an electric razor so you don't cut yourself shaving.

We waited for Bob to contact us but he didn't. That should have been a warning, but everyone was so busy.

Poor Mum had to cook for this lot but she didn't mind. Tabitha and I helped her and so did some of the new ones.

Grandpa and the Vampires practised day and night. It was a good thing there were no neighbours to disturb. Ma said that spoiled the fun but I don't think she really meant it.

And Dad was especially busy, rushing here and there, arriving and departing in a chauffeur-driven Mercedes and making long phone calls. For everything had to be just so for the big event, Grandpa and the Vampires first (and last) live concert.

CHAPTER 28

I'd been anxious about taking Frank to the concert. Hurling himself at big Drac like that hadn't done him any good. And although his lordship had sent the formula off to the laboratory to have a year's supply manufactured it had not yet arrived. So Frank was beginning to look a bit like a rag doll.

There's never been a pop concert like it they say. And they're right. Take my word for it, I was there. But I expect you read about it in the papers anyway.

We had seats towards the back. Why was that? After all, I could have had my pick of seats. Well, we had Frank with us and we were keeping our heads down. Even with his head down Frank stuck out, he was so tall. And he kept sucking his thumb. "Don't do it Frank," I said. "People will look at you and it puts a strain on your hand too. You know what'll happen if you're not careful."

The warm-up group went off, and there was a great roar as the main attraction came on, his lordship first with Ma in her slinky red dress, and then Josh and Sandra followed by Bag, Charlie and Freddie. They had their vampire outfits on, long cloaks and fake teeth and so on.

I looked at the long curtain behind them at the back of the stage. Behind the curtain? We weren't going to see that. Ma and Dad would have made sure. But half way through the second number it happened. On electronic rollers the curtain slowly peeled back.

Grandpa and the Vampires hadn't a clue what was going on. The curtain silently drew across the stage. And behind the curtain a huge mirror that reflected everything on the stage in a gigantic exaggeration for the audience's delight.

It took a while for the murmuring to get going. Then shouting and a few screams. Ma looked back first. Her voice cut right through the music. "Oh mi gawd!" she said, and they all turned. The music stopped. For a moment they all stood, backs to the audience, looking at the empty mirror. Then they were gone, legging it off stage, and pandemonium broke out.

We hurried to the dressing room. Inside, Dad was tearing his hair out, and the Scurfs were collapsed in gloom. Even his lordship. I'd never seen him so gloomy. Boris put his head round the door. "What are we to tell them?" he said. "The Theatre Manager is here".
His lordship looked dreadful. "It's over," he said.
"Not it's not." It was Tabitha speaking. "You guys get back on stage."
"Huh," said Dad. "They'll be torn to bits and then sent to the zoo."
"Not if you handle it right," said Tabitha, and explained her idea. After a minute I could see she was right, and after two or three minutes more she had convinced everyone.

"Can you do it?" said his lordship to Dad. I saw there was a sparkle in Dad's eyes.

First stop was the Manager. "I'm so sorry," said Dad. "We should have told you, but it had to be a complete surprise to everyone. Get them all into their seats and there'll be an announcement."

Next, Dad, Boris and I went to the control room. The lights, curtain and so on were operated from there. As we approached I thought I saw Bob's back vanishing round a corner. Inside the room we stood over a shifty looking technician while the curtain was moved back. Boris stayed on after us for a few minutes. "I'd better frighten him a bit, a lot," he said.

We got back to our seats just as Dad came on stage. There were catcalls at first but he waited for silence. "My friends," he said. "Our secret is out. Grandpa and the Vampires are real vampires. Now, they're most upset it's all come out. But nonetheless they will continue with the concert provided you promise to keep their secret. Do you?"

As the audience shouted its reply Boris and Levin dashed on stage and pretended to bite Dad. They'd dressed up in vampire outfits with fake teeth and lots of fake blood. They smeared more fake blood on Dad who staggered around the stage and fell down and they pulled him off by his legs. As they did so Grandpa and the Vampires entered from the other side.

260

It was the only live concert they did, but if they'd done one hundred it would have been the best. After seven encores the audience gave up and went home. We lost Frank in the crush and it took ages to find him. In fact I'd decided he must have fallen to bits at last and was directing my gaze to the floor when I bumped into him. He said, "I dun see the big man drive off with that Bob person." It was clear who had been behind the removal of the curtain.

We were exhausted. I could see there was going to be no party tonight. His lordship said to me, "I suggest you and Tabitha stay at your parents' and get a good night's sleep."
"What about Frank?" I said.
"The ointment arrives tomorrow morning" he replied.
"He'd better come with us."

Dad was on the phone all next morning. Most of the calls were from the press. There were a lot of "no comments" from Dad. He said, "Apparently they say it's the best publicity stunt for years." He also had some long phone calls from his lordship and by lunch time he seemed very preoccupied.

Tabitha went off to her parents after lunch. About teatime, Dad said, "We'd better drive to his lordship's". We chatted on the way. "What if the papers get hold of that technician and get his story?" I asked.
I don't think so," replied Dad. "His lordship sent Boris round this morning to talk to him, with a wad of bank notes and a pre paid voucher for an expensive funeral."

261

"But they'll be able to look at the mirror" I said.

Dad shook his head. "No. As a rich old vampire and a rich pop megastar his lordship has certain advantages. He bought the theatre this morning. The mirror is being replaced this afternoon."

"And what about Big Drac?" I said.

"Igor and his men went round to fix him this morning," said Dad, "but he's gone into hiding. The house is empty and has a for sale sign up."

"Then what about Bob?"

"We mishandled Bob," said Dad. "We'll just have to live with the result. So long as Vladimir is free, Bob will have a supply of blood from him. At least we don't have to worry about that." So Bob was free to make more trouble, which he did but that's another story.

As we drove down the drive I knew something was wrong. The front door was wide open and the house was silent. There was no one in the kitchen. There was no one in any room. The house was empty. They had all gone.

CHAPTER 29

A note had been left on the kitchen table. It just said "My dear Egbert, Another surprise. I'm sorry not to have forewarned you before this morning. I will be in touch."

I found a note hidden under my pillow. It was from Frank, written by Freddie. Freddie wasn't too good at writing, especially when he was out of his face on blood. It said, "dere Eg, we got to go. Its secret. My stuff came today. I love you. Frank." There was a squiggle where Frank had tried to write his name. And that was that.

Over the next months, letters came via Igor, who removed the outer envelope so you couldn't see where they'd come from. And we had some phone calls. Dad knew where they were, but he wouldn't tell me. "You'll have to wait," he said

I passed my exams with good grades, all that I'd hoped for and received a big congratulations card signed by each of the band. But that was all. The end of the holidays was on the horizon. I'd just got to the point where I was beginning to miss Big Drac when Dad showed me a letter from his lordship.

"We would like you to visit us if you will. You and I have a lot of business to catch up on and we all miss all of you. Bring young Tabitha if you can and if her parents will let her come. I enclose four tickets. When you get there present yourself to the station master's office."

The tickets were to Edinburgh. The people in the station master's office were very helpful when we got there. They gave us another envelope. In it a letter said, "Go to MacGregor's Car Hire in Fulton Street and identify yourselves."

"Och," said the man when we got there. "I'll get Angus." Angus silently drove us in a northerly direction for hours. Finally he stopped by a quayside, unloaded our luggage and departed in more silence. Before he left he gave Dad an envelope.

Inside it said, "Take the ferry. On the other side, ring McSporran and say who you are." And it gave a phone number. It was dusk. I peered through the gloom and saw a small ferry coming across the water.

McSporran communicated in grunts and talked to himself in a foreign language. He took us across the island in his battered old car. The moon had come out and it was a bright still night. A single track road took us to a deserted cove and we drew up by a small pier.

By the pier was a boat and by the boat was Boris. "How nice to see you Mr. Egbert," he said. He spoke to McSporran in a strange language and gave him something.
"What's that language?" I asked.
"Gaelic, Mr. Egbert," he said. "His lordship lived for some years north of Inverness but we had to move on. That was a long time ago."

As the boat chugged its way, a dark shape began to appear on the horizon. As we approached the rocky island I could see the outline, on a hill top, of a rambling Scottish castle. "Home," said Boris.

CHAPTER 30

We arrived just after breakfast and to a warm welcome. Frank rushed towards me as I entered. Having a toddler jump up and put his arm round your neck is one thing. But Frank was six feet tall and his version was more like all in wrestling.

While I was wondering what had hit me Frank picked up a book that had been carefully laid by the front door in readiness. "Look Eg, look," he said. The book had a picture and one word per page. "Gran'pa is learning me to read," he said proudly, and turned to the page for capital E. There was a picture of an egg. "Look it's got your name here." Then he looked a bit cross. "I don't have my name nowhere," he said.

Frank couldn't stop talking. "This ointment's reel good," he said, "An' I can have as much as I want. I've bin out training with Bag. An' I take Freddie out for walks an' I dun use a knife and fork last week."

His lordship greeted us. He was wearing a kilt. I noticed Boris was too. His lordship said "We must adapt. I give compulsory gaelic lessons three times a week to everyone."

I asked Boris how his lordship had arranged it all so quickly. "On the contrary," he said. "He planned it months ago when he saw the advertisement for the sale of the island following the death of the old Laird. The climate at our old home had become too hot in more ways than one."

"So that's why he wasn't worried when it was burnt down."

Boris nodded his head. "Everything we wanted had been moved out the day before." He laughed. "The only thing that worried us was that there might not be enough of us to run the island properly." As they say, every bite has a silver lining.

Ma was full of energy. "Hoots young Eg," she slapped me on the back. "Och aye, I'm a bloomin' farmer's wife now." There were cows and sheep. Ma loved it. "We're gonna make our own bread an' veg an' all. An' Charlie, 'es gone organic. Out all night weedin' and then doin' the milkin' before 'e goes ter bed. An' not a year ago 'e fought milk was somefink like coca cola. 'E weren't 'alf tickled pink when 'e found it come out of cows.

It seemed Big Drac had recruited a lot of talent. He and Aunt Agnes had chewed their way through two agricultural students, three cooks, a carpenter, an electrician and a teacher of sociology and psychology. So Josh's studies wouldn't be interrupted. That pleased Sandra. Josh didn't seem to mind. "I can take a long view," he said. "I've got years ahead." My little brother! Josh's idea of a long view used to be standing on top of a hill.

I asked Boris if there were only vampires on the island. "Yes," he said, "except for McHaggis. He's the retired butler of the old Laird. He'd stayed on as caretaker after the Laird's death and he asked his lordship for a job. His lordship took a fancy to him and said you realise we're all vampires, don't you?

267

McHaggis said the old Laird had sucked his blood for fifty years and he was sure anything his lordship offered must be an improvement."

That night we had a banquet. A whole sheep on a spit. Ice cream. Blood and whisky cocktails all round, well nearly all round. At the end Charlie, Josh and Bag played a number on the bagpipes.
Ma was really proud. "Our Charlie's writin' a bagpipe concerto," she said.
I asked Bag if they were still going to play as a group. "Yea," he replied. "Not 'alf. We're puttin' in a studio and one of this new lot is goin' off ter train as a sound engineer."
Later Dad said, "Sales are booming but no live shows or interviews !"

Speaking of interviews, Boris told us his lordship had made enquiries about Bob. Apparently Bob was really horrid. He'd never got married and didn't have any friends, not proper friends anyway. His hobby was his work and he particularly liked pulling people apart on his programme: not literally although he might have liked that too. So it looked as if Big Drac had found a real companion.

We stayed a week and we had a wicked time. When we left, his lordship said, "I am indebted to you. Can I persuade you to join us?" And then we both laughed, for we knew the answer. I would miss them all, especially Frank. "I'll always be your best friend," he said.

268

And so I went back with Mum and Dad and Tabitha to my own world. But if I'd known the trouble we were all going to get from Big Drac and Bob I might just have considered the offer.

THE END